LIZ LOVELOCK

MY FORBIDDEN GUY

MY GUY #3

Cover Design by Ben Ellis from Be Designs
Photographer: Reggie Deanching from The Stable & Models of RplusMphoto
Models: Ryan Stacks and Anna Harmon
Edited by Anna from Creating Ink
Proofread by Jen Lockwood Editing
Formatted by Tami at Integrity Formatting

www.lizlovelockauthor.com

MY FORBIDDEN Guy ♡

MY GUY #3

CHAPTER

I'm standing on Crow's Peak while Elsie freaks the hell out. The wind blows around me, and all I can say is that I'm glad I'm not the one in her position. Elsie wrings her hands as she glances at the drop from the nook in the side of the cliff then spins away. From here, it doesn't seem like anything to be worried about, but being on the edge would be another thing entirely.

Aiden reaches to take her hand, and they exchange some words.

"You going to jump?" Dane steps beside me, shirtless. My heart swims with excitement.

I turn to face him. He mirrors my movement. We step into each other. There are only inches between us. His large, toned arms weave around my waist and pull me against him. Now there's only a breath between us. He leans and presses his lips to mine. It's like I'm on a roller coaster, and with each kiss, my stomach flips.

Pulling back slightly, I say, "I wasn't planning on it, but if you do it with me, I might consider it."

He pulls his bottom lip between his teeth. "Do you think that's such a good idea? You know, with Parker being here?"

Therein lies the problem. Dane is one of Parker's best friends, and of course, being Parker's younger sister, technically I'm off-limits.

I shrug. "He'll probably just think you're being kind to his kid sister." I hate this. The whole situation. Why should we be afraid of being together? Well, we're not *officially* together. It's more... friends with benefits. *Really* good benefits.

"We need to be careful. I told you he warned me away from you just last Monday."

Ah, yes, I remember that. Too bad for Parker.

This thing between Dane and me has been going on since he and Addison got together—I think maybe two months or something like that. Because it's not anything solid, I've not kept track. I've become good at keeping secrets.

Elsie's high-pitched scream rings out as she takes the plunge. I turn just in time to catch their bodies slip from my view. *Damn, she's brave.* I'm wearing my scaredy pants today. I didn't sign up for this jumping-off-a-cliff business.

But while standing here in Dane's arms, nothing is impossible. "With regard to Parker, I think we should consider telling him," I say.

Voices sound behind me, and Dane drops his arms from around me. The loss of his touch hits me.

"Paislee, come jump with me," Elsie calls as she comes

up the stairs from the beach at the bottom of the cliff. I turn back to Dane, and sadness rips through my chest. He won't tell Parker.

I move away from him and walk toward Elsie and Addison. Rocks crunch under my feet; it's all I can hear. *What am I going to do?*

"What's wrong?" Addison asks when I stop where a bag with multicolored towels sticks out on a bench under a large shady tree. I drop myself onto the seat with a loud sigh.

Aiden and Parker are still in the water. My gaze drifts over to where I left Dane. His head is low. It's like a switch flick—he looks up and races toward the stairs to make his way down to where the guys are.

"I think Dane and I are going nowhere," I finally reveal.

They lay out their towels and sit on them, facing me.

Addison reaches for a packet of potato chips and pops it open. Shoving one in her mouth and waiting a moment to finish chewing, she says, "Look, like I said, tell Parker."

"I would, but Dane doesn't want to. What am I supposed to do? Force him?"

Elsie purses her lips, the natural gloss she wears shining in the sun. "I think that's not a bad idea. Stick it to him. It's not just him who gets to make the decisions in this relationship."

"I wouldn't say it's an actual relationship," I mutter, leaning over to take a handful of chips from the packet.

"Oh, I thought you were." Addison's eyes widen.

I shake my head. "No. Only friends with benefits."

"Damn, that's got to suck. I'm not sure what to do. I would want him to be truthful with his friend and your brother," Elsie says.

"I think my sister is a chicken."

All three of our heads whip around at Parker's voice.

I throw more chips at him, laughing. "Shut up. I'm not stupid, and I don't have a death wish."

"Dane told me he offered to jump with you—you should have taken him up on it."

My focus flicks to Dane, standing behind Parker, a small grin on his face.

"Your new nickname is Chicken," Parker says.

"Gee, you're a bunch of children. Chicken? Really? You're going to have to come up with something better than that." I roll my eyes at the silly nickname.

Parker shrugs. "You're stuck with it now, Chicken Little."

"I can deal with it, Little Bro." I hold my fingers up, indicating the size of something important to him. The group bursts out laughing.

"Ouch." Parker holds his hand to his chest. I catch Dane staring in my direction. There's something in the way he keeps a grip on my gaze. I pull my bottom lip between my teeth and cock an eyebrow. He shakes his head, but there's no way he can hide that smile—the one that makes me want him even more.

CHAPTER
Two

"Hey, what are you thinking about?" Dane shifts and I lift my head off his firm chest. I stare into his beautiful chocolate-swirl eyes and run my fingers through his longish hair. Damn, he takes my breath away. His hand comes to my cheek briefly then brushes some stray sandy-blonde strands away from my face. Closing my eyes, I relish the touch.

I lift my chin on my hand resting on his body. "I was thinking about when we first met."

Dane chuckles. "You acted like this stuttering little schoolgirl."

"Shut up." I smack his bare stomach, laughing. He flinches.

Dane becomes silent. His eyes bore into mine. "You captured my heart the moment Parker introduced us. All I can say is that I'm glad you didn't give up on us, even if it meant keeping things from Parker." It's like a rope has been placed around my torso and pulled. The tightness uncomfortable.

I had wanted to tell Parker about us, but after some heated discussions, we both agreed it was best if we didn't, and now here I am, lying in Dane's bed, with my brother down the hall. An uneasy heaviness begins to weigh down my stomach.

I open my mouth to respond when voices echo outside Dane's door. Our heads whip around. The voices become louder.

"He should be up by now," Parker yells from the hallway. Before I can manage to scramble up, Dane sits and brings me with him. His hands touch my side, and he shoves me off the bed like someone would do to their dirty laundry. The wind leaves my lungs as I face-plant onto the carpeted floor. My cheek stings from the impact. I go to stand and give Dane a piece of my mind when his door flies open. I press my body as close to the floor as I can, even hold my breath, just in case.

If Parker stays at the door, I won't be seen from where he's standing. I'm wedged between the wall and the bed.

"Get up. We've got training in thirty minutes."

"Yeah, who could miss you yelling down the hall?" Dane bites back as if he's just been woken up. *Please don't walk into the room.*

"Shut up and get up." Parker laughs.

The door slams shut, and I bounce off the floor like it's spring-loaded.

"Sorry," Dane whispers as he rushes off the bed, his arms open. His brows pinch together, worry glimmering in his eyes.

Holding out my hands, I stop him. "Don't. Perhaps this—whatever it is—has run its course. I'm not the kind of girl who deserves to be kicked off the bed and forced to hide out on the floor," I grit through clenched teeth. Saying I'm angry wouldn't even begin to describe the pulsating rage that burns through my veins. I'm hurt. So hurt and ashamed. I blink furiously, hiding the wetness clouding my vision.

"No, Pais, please don't do this. I'm so sorry. I panicked." He grabs my arm, but I shove him in the chest. I pick up my flip-flops and bag off the ground in the corner of the room.

Pulling my bag strap over my head, I turn to Dane. His pained gaze stares back at me.

"Look, yes, I'm pissed and hurt. Maybe you need to think about what it is you really want, and if I'm one of those things. Then, perhaps we need to make this official and tell Parker."

His eyes widen.

When he remains silent, I say, "I'll give you some time to think about it."

Again, he doesn't say anything and lets me walk out the door.

I dart across to the bathroom opposite Dane's room. This is usually my escape route.

"Pais?"

I pause mid-step, turning. It's Addison. I heave a sigh of relief. *It's her.*

"What are you doing here?" Her voice is low. "Parker's here."

I spin and spy him coming out of his room down the hall. *Dammit.* "Hey, Paislee. What are you doing here?"

My heart hammers against my chest. My mind is blank—all my excuses evade me. "Oh, I'm just—"

"She was meeting me. I asked her to come here before we went and grabbed a bite to eat." Addison smiles sweetly at Parker, who simply shrugs and walks past us.

"Okay, have fun. I'll see you after classes." He kisses her and turns to leave.

I want a relationship like that: where the participants are open, honest, and not afraid to show the world.

"See you," Addison and I say in unison. Then, her heavy stare turns to me.

Dane's door flies open, and he appears surprised to find us standing there. "Catch you later." He drops his gaze and moves around us.

Great, now I've made things super awkward.

"Perfect," I mutter. Moments ago, everything was great, and now I don't even know where I stand.

CHAPTER
Three

In the courtyard, my focus is on my phone. Dane had messaged me to meet him here at midday. I have an ache in my stomach. I already know what this is about. The lump in my throat blocks the sobs for now. I don't want to work myself up if I've read the entire situation wrong.

My head tips up and my breath leaves me as Dane makes his way toward me. His dark eyes are lowered; there's still hurt there. He shouldn't be the one hurt. I was the one put out like a feral cat. His mouth is turned down. The guy who usually brightens my day is about to destroy me—I can tell by the look on his face.

He comes to a stop in front of me. He doesn't make any attempt to reach for me. I ache to throw myself at him and forgive him for this morning. I need to be strong. It's always been a possibility that things wouldn't work between us. I desperately want them to, though.

"Hey," he says, his voice low and void of emotion.

"Hey, what's wrong?" I swallow my fears and try to get this sorted as quickly as possible—rip the Band-Aid off.

Dane's eyes fall to the ground. My heart plummets to the pavement with a resounding crack. I'm sure everyone around us heard my heart break.

Tears brim in my eyes as reality sinks in. It's not how I thought this would play out. My hand furiously brushes away the escaping drops. It was only this morning that I put the choice to him. I thought he'd choose me.

"Why?" I can't help the hiccup that seizes my throat.

Dane stares at me. His face is an unreadable mask. I want to stomp my feet and throw a massive tantrum, but he chose a public place to do this for a reason. No doubt so he wouldn't be able to hold me, and I wouldn't be able to try to hug him.

He tugs at his backpack straps sitting over his shoulders. I drink in his appearance like it's the last time I'll be able to partake of his particular flavor. His white tee clings to his washboard body, and his basketball shorts hang on his hips. And then there's *that hair*. As if he knows what I'm thinking about, he reaches up before running his fingers through his dark-brown waves. I want to run my fingers through it again.

"We shouldn't have to hide this." He gestures between us. "It's for the best," he mutters again, as though he's trying to convince himself. He turns to leave; his step falters. My feet automatically move to him, hoping he glances a look back to me and tells me this is all a joke. His shoulders drop. He walks away slowly at first and then his stride picks up.

I'm left standing in the courtyard. People stream past me, oblivious to my heartbreak.

I stare at Dane's back as he walks away, taking my heart

with him. Does he even care how much this hurts? I collapse onto the bench. Thankfully, it's here to catch me, because now he isn't. How could he do this to me? This is my own fault, I guess. I pressured him. Perhaps I should have left things the way they were. The question is, would I have been happy to continue like that? The answer would be no. No relationship should be kept a secret. It should be sung from the rooftop of the tallest building.

I honestly thought we had something special, but now it's ended and all because he's my brother's friend. It hasn't been a problem for the last couple of months and all those nights I spent with him.

Staring around at people and their happy, smiling faces, I want to slap them and say, "How can you be happy when I can't be?" I hate them and their stupid cheerfulness.

"Hey, Pais." Addison's chirpy voice pulls me back to reality. I turn to her. Her face scrunches with concern. "What's wrong?"

Her backpack falls to the pavement, and she sits beside me. Her arm comes around my shoulders and pulls me into her. I can't help my tears now; they pour and don't stop. My hands come to my face to hide my emotions from onlookers.

"What's going on?" Parker's voice is full of concern.

If he finds out it's about one of his friends, there's no telling what he'll do. Most likely, he'll turn into a full overprotective big brother.

Clearing my throat, I pull my heavy head from Addison's shoulder and look up at Parker. "I've got some painful women cramps." I swipe away the fresh tears that drop onto my cheeks as the lie slips easily from my mouth. Addison holds me tightly against her. I think she knows I'm lying.

Parker shifts his feet uncomfortably. "Well, ah, okay.

Addison, I'll catch up with you later." He leans over, and I hear them kiss—I don't dare look. More water fills my eyes as I remember I won't be able to kiss Dane anymore. From the way he made me feel in those special moments between us, I thought he'd try harder to make us work. Well, we had been working, but now it's over.

"What's really going on?" she whispers in my ear.

I stand. "I don't want to talk about it here."

"Okay." Addison hooks her arm through mine, collects her bag, and starts pretty much dragging me along with her.

"Where are we going?" I ask.

"Back to my dorm, and you're going to spill the beans on what's wrong."

How can I argue with her?

She pushes open her door and pulls me through the doorway. My entire body slowly loses feeling. My mind and body are numb. Dane has officially broken the usually happy Paislee. He's taken away the one thing I constantly crave—him.

Addison eases me onto the couch. Then, she walks away from me, only to return moments later with a box of tissues and all the junk food she could, apparently, find in the dorm.

I raise my eyebrows. "What, do you keep a special box with all this type of stuff in it?" I ask, my voice not sounding like my own.

She chuckles. "We have a sugar shelf in the pantry. We each buy something to go on there every week. It's our emergency stash for breakups, exam weeks, our monthly visitors, you name it." She pauses for a second, and her stare makes me shift in my seat. "What's going on?"

Her question suffocates me. If I say it, then it makes it too real. I don't want it to be.

Her door swings open, and Elsie flies in like a woman on a mission, dropping her bag by the door then kicking it shut. The slam is enough for me to jump.

"Oh my goodness, I'm so glad I found you both. Are you alright, Pais?" She rushes to my side. Her breaths heavy like she ran the whole way here.

I cock an eyebrow. "Were you looking for me?"

"Yes. I was just at the boys' house when Dane came barreling through the door. He looked like he wanted to pick a fight with Aiden."

Addison sucks in a sharp breath behind me.

My hand flies to my mouth. "Did he tell you what he was angry about?"

She nods, a solemn expression on her face. "I'm so sorry, Pais. You watch; he'll come to his senses. He just needs to wake up to himself and tell Parker, then all will be good."

Addison stands. "Wait, what? Did something happen between you and Dane?"

The stone is lodged back in my throat, and tears fill my eyes. "He said it was for the best. I mean, can you believe that? Am I not good enough anymore? I would have spoken to Parker. Sure, he might have been angry at the start, but I'm sure he would have gotten over it." The words spew from my mouth.

Addison parks her bum on the coffee table and takes my hands in hers. "Girl, it's his loss. He's the one not seeing what's right in front of him."

"What's the point? It's all over, and now I have to move on. I don't want to be a stage-five clinger. That's not who I am. Today, I'm going to drown my sorrows in all the sugary goodness, and then tomorrow I'll start again." I try to sound strong, but inside, I'm a crumbling mess. It's going to take some time to let go of this numbness that's seeped into my body.

"Don't worry. We're here for you," Elsie reassures me, rubbing my back.

"Yes. We can hate on Dane together," Addison says. The girls laugh. I can only manage a half-smile. They mean well. Today is simply not my day for jokes.

"I still can't believe he didn't even try to fix it. That's what makes me the angriest. It's as though he simply wanted it over and done with—to wipe his hands of me."

"No, I'm sure that's not the case," Elsie says.

A look passes between them. They're not so sure themselves.

I wish today had never happened. Can I rewind to this morning and change the entire situation?

CHAPTER
Four

"Are you going to come to the basketball court?" Addison asks as she stands from the brown, worn leather couch. It's obviously seen better days. It reminds me of something from the 80s.

Shaking my head, I say, "It's probably for the best that I stay away. It's still a little raw, and seeing him will hurt even more."

Elsie and Addison nod.

"You're welcome to stay here and eat all this." Addison gestures to all the open treats on the table. Peanut butter—I would usually eat it by the spoonful—chocolate kisses, and something called Nutella. Aiden had given it to Elsie to try, and she'd brought it back for the sugary shelf.

"It's okay. I think I'm just going to go home and try to sleep away this dreadful day." I bury my head in my hands.

"How am I supposed to act around him now? Just like before, only with a little more distance and no touchy-feely?"

Elsie snorts.

"What? I'm serious. I don't know how I'm supposed to hang around you both and the guys and not feel hurt when he starts dating other girls."

"Perhaps, when you feel up to it, you could give online dating a go," Elsie suggests.

"Elsie," Addison hisses, her eyes wide as she takes a small swipe at Elsie's arm.

"It's okay. Good thought, though I'm not sure my mother would approve of something so unsafe." She would lose her mind if she found out I'd done that.

My phone beeps with a message. I reach for my bag on the floor where I'd dropped it when I was dragged here a couple of hours ago. A message from Dane stares back at me.

Dane: Hey, I just wanted to check and see how you are?

Is he kidding?

"It's a message from Dane," Addison states as she turns back and ties her sneakers.

"How could you tell?"

"Your face went from soft to all scrunched up. I only need one guess who could cause that reaction." Addison shrugs.

"You're good," I say. "He's asking how I am."

"Don't answer him," Elsie shouts as she exits the living area and heads to her bedroom. "You need to make him crawl and beg," she yells.

I stare at the screen, not sure what to do.

The girls now have their shoes on and their bags slung over their backs.

"Crawl and beg. Do you think?" I ask, glancing at Elsie.

She takes her hair and gathers it together, tying it with a hair tie. Her hands then land on her hips. "Well, it will tell you if he's really ready to let what you both had go. Or he'll come to his senses and do what needs to be done." Elsie shrugs.

I lock my phone and shove it back in my bag. "You're right. He can suffer with the guilt for a while. I don't need him." I stand, somehow finding my strength even with a fragile heart.

"You go, girl," Elsie cheers. Addison whoops loudly.

"You pair are crazy. Thanks for the afternoon. I think I'm going to go home, and I'll try to figure out my next move." I collect my bag and bid my farewells.

When I step out of their building, darkness is starting to fill the sky. It feels like it's taking over me too. Loss tugs at my chest. I hate this empty feeling.

I officially have no sneaking around to do tonight. No plans with anyone. Mom is working, so I'm pretty safe if I go home. I won't get the twenty questions.

I pull into our driveway. We aren't a rich family—my mother has worked too hard to give Parker and me everything we've ever needed. She's shown us what hard work can get you. She's now a doctor at the hospital. I admire her for all she has achieved.

My father is never a topic of conversation inside the walls of this house. All I know is that he left when I was young. I'd never given him much thought until these past twelve months. What kind of person he is and if he has another family. Could I possibly have more brothers or sisters? I've never been one to shy away from asking Mom something, but doing this would be a betrayal to her after all she's done for us.

After scrounging around for something that interests me for dinner, I finally sit down. Turning on the television, I see an episode of *Blue Bloods* has just started. *Perfect*. I love this show. Give me a Jamie over a Danny any day. Jamie is soft, caring, and shows compassion—very similar to Dane. Danny, on the other hand, is a hardhead and often hates being told what to do. I'm not sure I could handle someone with his personality.

My phone dings. Perhaps I'll leave it for tomorrow. I don't want to see another message from Dane tonight.

I need to know who it is, though.

> **Addison:** Dane was moody tonight. Would it make you happy to know he seems miserable? It was like he was looking for you when we arrived.
>
> **Paislee:** Good. It serves him right.
>
> **Addison:** Thought that might make you feel better.
>
> **Paislee:** I can't say it makes me feel better. I'm sad and lonely now.

Lonely Paislee. Story of my life.

My phone sounds off again.

> **Addison:** Naw... don't think like that. How you're feeling will pass. When the time is right, you'll get back out there and start dating again.

I sure as hell am not going to be dating again any time soon.

> **Paislee:** Perhaps I'll become a nun. Lol.
>
> **Addison:** Now that's something I'd pay to see.

For the rest of the night, I'm left to my own thoughts.

No more messages. Just silence.

CHAPTER
Five

My eyes snap open. The TV is still going. I must have dozed off.

Was today a dream? Or did Dane actually end things?

I lift my arm to look at my watch and groan. Three in the morning. Damn, a pinch in my neck is giving me hell. After clicking off the television, I put my plate from my makeshift dinner in the sink and drag my blurry-eyed self to my room.

I've pinched myself a hundred times, hoping that I'm dreaming, but disappointment soon follows. Lying on my bed, I'm thankful Mom is doing the late shift. I don't want to go into details with her about my morose state.

Any other night I would have gone to the guys' house simply to hang out and also try to spend some time with Dane. Now, I don't think I'll be going near their place, or the boys, for a while. I don't want to risk running into Dane.

I twist my body toward my nightstand, grabbing my phone and rereading Dane's message from earlier—the nerve of him. How could he think for a second that I'd be okay? I'm so far from it that I don't ever want to go back to school and run the risk of bumping into him. He has ripped my heart out and mashed it up, all the while oblivious to the fact that I was falling in love with him.

I reread his message. My thumbs glide over the keyboard of the phone.

> **Paislee:** No, I'm not okay. Leave me alone. You chose this.

I hover over the send button. What would hurt him more? To reply or not to reply—that's the question. I read the above messages, and my heart fractures a little more.

> **Dane:** I miss your beautiful smile. Come see me tonight.

That was the message he'd sent me last night before I'd raced out of here, lying to Mom about where I was going. I'd sneaked in Dane's window, as I'd done plenty of times before.

I huff out a long breath then scroll back to his last message, sent hours ago. My reply still sits, waiting. My thumb hits send and that's that.

It's time to move forward.

My eyes spring open to my alarm rattling my tired and emotional brain. Rolling over, I search blindly for the spot on my phone to shut it off. I manage to lift my eyelid just enough until I see the little button on the screen. I press it then collapse back onto the pillow.

It's been an entire week of nothing. No more texts. No more visits to Parker's house. No more Dane. I miss him so much. I've been dragging myself out of bed at dawn to go for a run. It clears my mind and reminds me that I don't need him—that I can survive this stage of my life. Heartbreak is a natural thing for everyone to experience. Although, hopefully only once in a lifetime.

Who am I kidding? Some people keep getting slapped stupid with heartbreak.

I pull on my short black running tights and a pink workout singlet before slipping my phone into the little pocket on my pants. Pockets are the best. Whoever invented them deserves a medal. I slip into my runners and then attach my headphones and make my way downstairs to grab a bottle of water.

I'm in such a rush to leave that I don't notice the dim light coming from the kitchen at first. I've been avoiding Mom for the last week because I haven't wanted to go into detail with her about Dane. *Mothers…*

"You've been avoiding me."

My head flicks up, and I jump. I clutch at my chest. She's like a ninja, this one.

"Geez, Mom, you scared the hell out of me." I think I still might have a heart attack with how fast it's racing.

She smiles while taking a small sip from her steaming cup of herbal tea. Mom is all about healthy living, which I totally get with her being a doctor and all. But that smell could clear a house of teenagers in a matter of seconds. "I notice when my kids avoid me, and that's you right now."

I sigh. Moving to the bench, I grab the bottle of water she pushes my way. "I'm just not ready to discuss things yet. By the way, that smells really bad."

Mom smiles, nodding, followed by another sip. She keeps her eyes on me. "It's good for you. And I understand if you don't want to talk to me yet."

One short sentence and I'm ready to spill everything. She has a way like that. It's *the stare*. It has to be. It's not a mean, tell-me-what-you-know stare. It's an if-I-hold-your-gaze-long-enough-you'll-tell-me look. It says, *I'm your mother; you can't keep secrets from me.*

"If I tell you, you can't tell Parker." I wave my finger in a disciplinary way, swearing her to secrecy.

"You know I'm a vault." She runs her index finger over her chest in the form of an *X*.

I scoff. "Mom, you're a terrible secret keeper."

"So, don't tell me." She shrugs.

"Yeah, and then I'll have you continually asking."

"Okay, so what's said right now doesn't leave this house." She holds out her pinky.

I smile. "Really, Mom? You're going for a five-year-old's promise?"

"Hey, it worked when you were younger." She waggles her pinky.

Rolling my eyes, I hook mine with hers. "Okay, so I've been seeing Dane secretly."

Her eyebrows raise, and she pauses mid-sip. Slowly, she places the mug down. "You and Dane, huh?"

I nod. "It's not a relationship, per se. It's been going on since Addison and Parker started hanging out. I stayed over one night at the house, and the next morning, I was nearly busted. I ducked behind the counter. I thought we were caught, but since we weren't, we kept it a secret."

"Why keep it a secret? I'm sure Parker would be happy for you both. Dane is a nice young man."

He is a nice young man. Or that was what I'd thought. "Anyway, about a week ago, he literally pushed me out of bed as Parker walked in the door. It wasn't like we were naked or anything. So, I told him, in not so many words, that I was tired of being his dirty little secret and that he needed to make a choice." My voice cracks.

"And he chose to end it—whatever it was you two had going on," Mom finishes.

I nod and attempt to swallow the lump that's formed in my throat. I drop hopelessly onto the stool beside me. Mom comes and stands next to me. She puts her arm around my shoulders and pulls me into her.

I don't want to cry. I was sure my tears were all dried up. I can feel them there, teetering, wanting to fall.

"Honey, I'm sorry," she says. Her softness warms my heart.

I shake my head. "It's okay. I just need to move on."

Mom hugs me tighter, and I look up at her.

"Enjoy your life and be happy. Don't spend your days wallowing and hoping the feelings you have will go away. Perhaps you have some unspoken words you need to tell Dane, and that might make the breakup more official and give you a sense of peace. Did you get to share your feelings about anything the last time you were together?"

"No. I guess I was still in shock. He sent me a message, and I told him to leave me alone. He decided to end things. Screw him." Bitterness drips from my words.

"I still think you need to tell him how you're feeling. What was his message?"

I sigh. "Just asking me how I am, and so I let him know I'm okay. What? Does he think I'm simply going to forgive him and play buddy-buddy friends with him? I don't think so." I wriggle out of Mom's grip and stand. "Sorry, Mom. I need to clear my head."

"That's okay, honey. I'm here if you need me."

"I know. Thank you."

Mom extends her arms, and I step into them again. She secures me against her. Her familiarity soothes my fractured heart but doesn't heal it. "Everything will work out how it's supposed to." Her words linger on my mind long after I leave the house. And that's exactly the problem. Maybe Dane and I aren't meant to be.

CHAPTER
Six

I love the silence of the library and the smell of paperback books. There are only myself and another five students scattered around the tables. Sitting here working on one of my assignments from English, I can't get what Mom said this morning out of my head. It really hit me. *'Enjoy your life and be happy. Don't spend your days wallowing and hoping the feelings you have will go away.'* How am I supposed to enjoy myself?

Leaning over, I grab my notebook and pen from my bag. I need to make a list—one to remind me why I don't need Dane.

For starters, he's a chicken because he wouldn't even talk to my brother. Secondly, he ended things without giving me a chance to fix it myself or even allowing me to talk to Parker. And third, he pushed me out of bed like I was nothing. I would have dropped down there myself, but the way that I was simply shoved aside because of his fear really angered me.

"Hey, Paislee."

I lift my head from the notebook. It's Jase, captain of the college football team. His usually tidy blond hair is all shaggy, and his blue eyes stare right at me.

"Hey, what are you up to?" We've never spoken before. Addison introduced us a while ago. I have been so focused on Dane that I've never really taken him in. Now, here he stands in front of me. He's wearing cream cargo pants with a fitted white polo shirt, his arms bulging at the sleeves. I sit here and actually focus on him. With no Dane distracting me… he's hot. *Damn.*

Is it too soon for me to be looking at another guy?

Jase gestures to a seat across from me. "Do you mind if I sit?"

I scramble to pull in my textbooks which I'd scattered over the table. I hadn't wanted anyone to sit with me. But how can I say no to him? "Yeah, sure. Sorry about the mess."

He chuckles. "It's all good. How have you been? I've seen you around but could never get up the nerve to come talk to you. You were always with your brother, Addison, her friends, and his."

He is right. At first, I was only with them because of Dane, but the girls welcomed me with open arms. There's no more *hanging with the boys,* though. That's all over.

"Yes, I've hung with them since I was new here. Now it's just easy." I shrug. Technically, it's not a lie.

"I hope you don't mind me coming to sit with you." He slides into the seat across from me. I stare right into his glittering blue eyes. I should have taken notice of him much sooner—it probably would have saved me all this current heartbreak.

"No, not at all. It's actually nice to have someone else to talk to—other than my brother's friends. Don't get me wrong. I love hanging out with Addison and Elsie. They're my people. The girls anyway." I laugh nervously. I clutch the pen in between my fingers and twist it around. It's then that I realize my notebook is wide open. I quickly shut it, hoping he didn't see what I had written down.

"That's good. I was wondering if you wanted to go on a date this weekend?"

My heart stutters at his random question. "Don't you have a game?" I'm sure they play most weekends. I don't keep up with football, so I might be wrong.

"We do. Did you want to come and watch and then we could grab something to eat before the party?"

I chew my bottom lip. A small silence builds between us as I think on his offer. Am I ready to date? It's only been a week.

I must have been quiet for too long when Jase interrupts my thoughts.

"If you don't want to, that's okay. It's a home game this week. Bring the girls if you want. Although, I'd much rather take you to grab a bite without them." He winks. My stomach swirls.

"I'd love to come and watch and then get some food." As I say the words, my unease builds. What if Dane sees us? I'm not sure I'm ready. What if I'm getting into something too soon? The dreaded what-ifs keep piling up.

"That's great. I'm looking forward to it. This is my number." He rises from the seat and comes around to where I'm sitting. I'm sure my mouth is hanging open. He takes the pen from between my fingers, then his warm hand takes mine and holds my palm open. I watch with awe.

He's really built—muscles upon muscles. I have to hold myself back from reaching out and touching them. I only want to see how firm they are. I'm sure I'll get a good look this weekend.

Jase finishes scribbling his number on my skin. Then, he holds out his hand. I take the pen from him and write mine down on his palm.

"Do you think I won't contact you?" I ask.

"I'm covering all my bases." His voice becomes low and gravelly as he leans over into my personal space. His hot breath tickles the exposed part of my neck. Tingles work their way slowly down my spine.

"Well, I look forward to hearing from you," I reply seductively.

Jase is very good at making the ladies swoon.

"Not unless I hear from you first." Jase cocks an eyebrow. His face seems so close. I'm staring at perfection. *Dane is perfect. I miss him.*

"You'll have to wait and see." A playful smile pulls across my face. I think this is going to be a game of cat and mouse. I need to talk to Addison or Elsie, or both of them. Their opinions, as bold as they are, are honest, and that's what I need.

Jase gives me a wink then pushes himself off the table and strolls away. I can't help it—I watch him. His perfect ass sits nicely in those pants. Dane's ass is impeccable. I loved grabbing it when he wasn't prepared. I smile at the memory. Dane is the only one who has ever taken my breath away. In my heart, I shouldn't let anything serious happen. My heart is still held by one man—*Dane*. I still want him even though he's done what he has.

I pull my phone from my bag and type a text out to Addison.

Paislee: I need you and Elsie. Can you meet me at the café?

It doesn't take long for her reply.

Addison: Be there in 10.

With that, I pack up all my stuff and head straight for the exit.

CHAPTER
Seven

"What's wrong?" Addison slides into the booth, followed by Elsie. I shove another fry in my mouth. They took longer than ten minutes; I had enough time to get food.

"What took you so long?" I ask as I push the basket of fries toward them to share.

They each take one, and then Elsie answers, "We got caught talking with the guys. Well, one guy in particular." She doesn't need to tell me who she is referring to.

"How is he?" I want to know.

A silent conversation happens between them, then Addison says, "He's miserable. Like, I've never seen him like this. I've not known him long, but he was always happy and chatty—unless that was your effect on him. He did ask how you have been."

This piques my interest. "What did you tell him?"

"The truth. That we haven't really seen you and that you were pretty upset by what he did. We kind of told him he'd made a stupid mistake. I think he knows that," Addison says.

I purse my lips and shrug. "He should have realized that when I was with him. Instead, he made a choice." Bitterness seeps into my words. I stuff three fries into my mouth for comfort.

"That's what we told him," Elsie says as she takes another fry from the basket.

"Anyway, forget about him for now. What did you want us for?" Addison asks.

I swallow my food then reply, "Jase asked me out on a date."

Both of their mouths pop open.

"Really?" Addison squeaks. Elsie coughs as though she's choking on her chips.

"Yes. He asked me to go watch his football game, get food, and go to the party together."

"This is great. What did you say?" Addison can't seem to hide her excitement.

"I said yes, but now I'm regretting it. It's too soon. It's only been a week," I plead.

"Jase is a great guy. It's not like you have to go jump into a relationship. You're only going on a date. Dane hasn't made much effort in reaching out to you, has he?" Addison gives me a stern look.

"I know, but I can't help feeling like I'm betraying him. We were never really together, but it felt like a relationship. We were whatever you want to call it for, like, two months. How am I meant to forget those feelings and go out with someone else when it's only been a week?" I am sure I sound pathetic.

Elsie reaches across the table and takes my hand. "Trust me when I say this is a good thing. If Dane sees you with someone else, it might give him the push he needs to stop being an idiot about everything. This will be great."

I'm not convinced. I'm not sure I can do this. Knowing that I'd hurt him hurts me. I can imagine his face right now if I did date someone else in front of him. His chocolate eyes would dim. This would wreck him.

I can see where Elsie is coming from, though.

"It's just a date. Nothing serious has to go on," Addison adds.

"Okay. I'll give it a go."

Their faces light up.

"Perfect. Let's hit the shops after classes today and find a new outfit," Elsie chimes in.

I roll my eyes. "I don't need a new outfit. I have plenty of clothes to wear." Elsie's bottom lip pokes out and her forehead pulls down. "The pout may work on Aiden but not on me." My phone vibrates in my bag. I'd turned it on silent for classes.

Jase: This is me. Just wanted to make sure no numbers got lost.

"It's him."

"What did he say?" Elsie asks, reaching over and attempting to grab my phone out of my hands. I pull it against my chest then turn it around and show them. Both have silly, wide grins on their faces.

"He's making sure this happens. No excuses now." Addison winks.

My heart sinks.

"Don't overthink things. It's only one date. It doesn't mean anything," Elsie assures me.

"Okay, I can do it." Even as I say the words, I don't believe them. I write a quick reply.

> **Paislee:** Well, that's lucky. I already washed my hands.

I smile at my reply. Seconds pass, and it's him again.

> **Jase:** I'm glad I got your number then. I'm looking forward to the weekend.

Elsie and Addison order more food and spend the next couple of hours chatting and catching up. I'm actually going on a date with Jase, captain of the football team.

Friday night is finally here. I've been an anxious mess all week. Addison and Elsie are at the point where they're simply tolerating me. I keep needing reassurance that I'm doing the right thing. There's still been nothing from Dane, which hurts and makes me angry.

"How does this look?" I step out of Addison and Elsie's bedroom in a pair of denim shorts and a fitted white shirt. Simple, yet sexy. I have a pair of black strappy shoes on, and hell, I've even painted my toenails a shimmery gold.

"Perfection," Elsie says as she sits on the couch. Addison nods, giving me a reassuring smile. I am anything but reassured right now. When things started with Dane and me, I don't even think I was as nervous as I am tonight.

"Thank you both for coming with me to the game. I need all the support." I run my hand over my shirt.

A knock at the door has us looking between each other. I'm not expecting anyone; were they? Elsie gets off the couch and pulls the door open. A spark lights my heart on fire. Dane stands in the doorway.

"Paislee, it's for you," Elsie responds dryly and walks into her bedroom.

I'm not sure I'm ready to talk to him. I sent him that message and that was the last I'd heard from him. It's been two weeks, and he's done nothing to reach out. No texts. Nothing.

Slowly, I walk on jelly-like legs toward him. His head hangs low, but the moment I begin my approach, he raises it, and I regret accepting this date tonight. His eyes swim with emotion. I have to fight the urge to run into his arms, to have him close, to get lost in him. "Hey," is all I can manage. My eyes can't leave him.

Dane rubs one of his arms. "Hey, I… ah, just wanted to check in and see how you were?"

"You're two weeks late," I snap, unable to hide the harshness of my words. I fold my arms across my chest, waiting to see what he comes back with.

"I know. You told me to leave you alone, so I wanted to give you some time."

Good answer. Still, I'm not sure. "I'm fine. Thanks for checking on me." A tightness tugs in my chest. I desperately want his arms around me, to feel his warmth. It's an ache that rips me apart inside.

"I am sorry about everything."

I frown. *Is he serious?* He wants to apologize *now?* The softness I was feeling toward him quickly does a flip. "I don't have time for this," I say in a clipped tone.

His eyes dance over my appearance. He shuffles his feet. "Just give me a minute. Please," he begs.

I sigh. "Fine," I practically growl, keeping my arms folded across my body.

"Pais, I know you're mad."

"That's an understatement," I interject.

He ignores me and continues. "I want to apologize for everything—for pushing you out of bed that morning and for not taking into consideration your thoughts and opinions on us." His feet move closer to mine. I catch his hand twitching, as if he wants to reach for me.

"There was no discussion. My opinion didn't matter; you made that clear. I was just a booty call to you. I get it."

"Please don't say that." He clears his throat. "You were so much more than that, and I know you know it despite us never putting a label on it. Would you give me another chance? Please?" There's desperation in his words. *He wants me back.*

I'm not sure that's a great idea. I'm certain to be the one who gets hurt again. My mouth forms a thin line, and I can't move my eyes from his. They look pained. An agonizing silence stands like a brick wall between us. It needs to come down. But I'm not sure I can let it fall yet.

"Are you ready to go, Paislee?" asks Addison. I turn to give her a small nod.

"Oh, you're going out?" He seems surprised. Maybe he expected me to still be wallowing at home with a broken heart. Well, I'm still suffering, but I couldn't sit here and wait for him to wake up to himself.

"Yes, Jase asked her out. We're going to watch the game and then they're going to get some food."

I want to die right now. With each word Elsie spoke, his face crumbled a little more. His eyes have become dark and low. He can't look at me.

"Sorry, we better get going," I say, ending the conversation.

Elsie hands me my clutch, and we all step out of the dorm. I reach for him and touch his arm. His head shoots up.

"See you later, Dane," I say.

He doesn't say anything, just waves. And I watch painfully as the guy I love stands in the hallway, and I'm sure that I've broken him even more than he broke me.

CHAPTER

Eight

I resist the urge to turn around. Elsie and Addison walk on either side of me. Wetness wells in my eyes.

I make it out of the building, and the minute I do, the tears won't stop.

"Oh, Pais, it's okay." Addison pulls me into her arms.

"I'm sorry. I know this is stupid," I blubber.

"No, he's the stupid one." Elsie rubs her hand on my back.

I step out of Addison's arms and brush away the dampness on my cheek. "Perhaps I should not go tonight." A part of me hopes they will agree.

"No, you're going. It's like Dane planned it. It's not your fault that on the night you're going on a date, he chooses that time to show up and tell you he misses you and he's sorry." Elsie doesn't stop firing her words. "He had his chance two weeks ago to reach out. He sent you one message and then chose to keep his distance. Don't let him ruin your night of fun."

As much as I want to get in my car and drive home, I won't. I miss Dane so much. I reluctantly nod, and we all keep walking.

Arriving down at the field, I'm nervous. I shouldn't be. It's not like this date with Jase has been broadcast over campus.

I follow the girls as they lead us to some seats. A few people shout out *hellos* to us. Some I don't know, but people know I'm Parker's sister. He's pretty well-known around campus.

I drop into a plastic chair with a sigh. I want to enjoy myself. But how can I when... well, *Dane?*

"Forget about him. Let's have fun." Elsie bumps my shoulder. I give a weak grin.

I finally take notice of where we're sitting. We're not far from the field, right beside the entrance and exit of our team.

A loud voice comes over the speaker, and then the music starts pumping. Our team runs out. I spot Jase right away as he's first to sprint onto the field. The crowd goes crazy for him.

Damn, he looks hot in his uniform. The red-and-white shirt hugs his already large frame. He's a wide receiver, and he's pretty freaking good at it.

I catch him scanning the seats. Is he looking for me? Surely not. I resign myself to the fact that he's just seeing how many people are here. There are a lot. I'm small compared to the crowd.

We chat for a bit while waiting for the game to start.

Addison goes and grabs some drinks and snacks. After a little while, the siren sounds and it's all systems go. I don't watch anyone but Jase.

I cringe every time he gets creamed into the ground. All I can think is that he's going to be sore tomorrow. This sport is rough.

When the game ends, we stay in our seats. I'm not sure where I was supposed to meet Jase. Stupid me should have asked before I came tonight. I haven't been as invested in this date as I should have been. I shoot off a quick message.

Paislee: I know I should have asked this sooner—where did you want me to meet you?

"Let's go wait outside. That game was a nail-biter. Those players must get so sore from the impact of those tackles," Elsie says as we walk out of the exit.

"I know! I cringed every time," I say, clutching at my chest. My phone goes off twice.

Jase: Just wait outside the exit closest to campus. I'll come find you. Did you enjoy the game?

Dane: Paislee, please. I know I made a mistake. Can you give me another chance, or can we at least be friends and talk again?

I reply to Jase first.

Paislee: Okay, I'm here. I enjoyed the game. You guys did really well. Great win.

"Girls, he said to wait at the exit closest to campus," I say. We find a spot and wait.

"Dane messaged me," I blurt out.

They both gawk at me.

"What did he want?" Elsie asks as she takes a seat on an empty bench.

I show them and Addison replies, "Just be his friend again. There's no harm in it."

I scoff. "Are you kidding me? It took everything in me tonight not to be the one begging him to take me back."

I start typing a message as the girls laugh at my expense.

Paislee: I'm not sure about another chance, but I'm happy to be your friend.

I can't hate him. I love him.

"What did you say?" Addison asks.

"I told him we could be friends. What else am I going to say—*No, don't talk to me again?*" I could have, but I don't want to. He is still something special to me. My first true love. I don't want to forget what we had. I know two months isn't a long time, but it's long enough for my heart to know what it wants. It wants him. If only he had put on his big-guy pants and spoken to Parker.

"You girls are going to the party, yeah?" I change the subject. I don't want to be left on my own at the house. I won't know anyone other than Jase.

Elsie answers, "Yeah, the boys are going to come." My heart leaps. Does that mean Dane is going to come too?

As though they read my thoughts, they both reply, "Don't."

I step back. My eyes are wide. "Are you two mind readers?" I can't help the laugh the escapes me. They join in.

"What's so funny?" a deep voice from behind startles me.

We all jump back and turn toward the speaker. It's Jase.

"Hey, sorry. We're being silly." I chew my bottom lip and avert my eyes.

Jase focuses on the faces behind me. "Hey, Addison. Hey, Elsie. Are you two coming with us to grab some food? You're welcome to."

Both of them greet him then decline his offer. We say our goodbyes, and I tell them I'll see them at the party later.

"So, what are you in the mood for?" Jase asks.

I lift a shoulder. "Anything. Surprise me." I smile.

He chuckles and throws his arm over my shoulders, tucking me in close to him. "Come on, beautiful. Let's get some food."

Okay, date time. Let's do this.

CHAPTER
Nine

*J*ase takes me to a place on the beach I've never been to before called Crabbies. I'm sure the teenagers these days give them hell for their business name. "Really? Who names their business this?" I gesture to the sign above me.

Jase laughs. "Yeah, it's unfortunate. They didn't think their business plan through. I can tell you the food is perfection. I hope you like seafood."

The hostess leads us to a booth. It's a quaint little place. The place has a rustic look to it. I'll have to bring the girls here. Pictures of fishermen holding their catches are spread over the blue walls. There's a kitchen area toward the back of the restaurant and a bar just in front of it. The cooks are prepping the large plates of food.

"Here are your menus." The hostess hands us an A4-

sized laminated sheet of paper. "Would you like to order some drinks?"

I order water, and Jase has the same.

"I'll be back shortly to take your meal orders." She gives us a smile and then goes to the front counter where she greets another couple.

Their menu is loaded with lots of seafood, which, thankfully, I love. "So, what's good here?" I ask while scanning.

"I like the surf and turf. Get it, turf for football and surf for the beach." I laugh.

Glancing up, our eyes lock and he smiles. It's infectious. I return one. My nerves seem to have disappeared.

"That was going to be my choice," I admit as I place the menu on the wooden table. He does the same.

Our drinks arrive, and the hostess sets a jug of water on the table as well.

Jase takes a large gulp from his. "So, Paislee, tell me about you. Of course, I know Parker, but I want to get to know you."

"I'm not sure there's much to tell. I can't say I'm that interesting." I shrug.

His pearly whites shine at me. "Don't give me that. So, why did you transfer here?"

Not many people have asked me that question. "I wanted to be with my family. What about you? How did you end up here?"

He leans back, stretching. Every vein in his neck pops, and all the muscles in his arms flex. I'm sure my eyes widen. "I got a football scholarship. I'm hoping to make it pro one day."

After watching him tonight, I have no doubt he'll make that dream a reality. He's a senior, so his time will be coming to an end here soon. "That's pretty cool. You'll do great. I have no doubt about it."

"What are your plans after college?" he asks as the server stops by to take our orders. "Two surf and turfs please."

She scribbles it down and leaves.

I twist the napkin in my hands. The question makes me nervous. "To be honest, I don't have any plans yet. I'm doing the basics for school, but I'm not sure where my heart is right now."

He nods as I speak. "I understand that. For a long time, I had no idea what I wanted, and then I played my first game and that was it. I knew without a shadow of a doubt that football was my future, and I've never looked back. Perhaps something will come to you soon."

His words are kind, and it makes me smile wider. He has put my mind at ease about my future so quickly. Not even my own mother has assured me as he did. "Wow, you're pretty smooth with your words."

His hand slides across the table and rests on top of my fidgety ones. The tingle his touch causes makes me stop. I'd completely forgotten I was twisting the napkin. I'd even started tearing it into little shreds. "It's okay. I'm not here to judge. I want to get to know you." He speaks low. There's a calming nature about him. It draws me to him.

The rest of the dinner passes pretty quickly. There's plenty of laughing, and we toss jokes at each other. Our meals are superb—I'll definitely be coming back.

When we leave, Jase wraps his arm around my waist. I'm not uncomfortable, but it doesn't feel right. Jase is a great guy—he's proven that to me tonight—always the gentleman. He would be the perfect boyfriend for any deserving girl—not me, though.

It's become clear tonight that there's only one person who can have my heart. *Dane.*

CHAPTER

Ten

*E*veryone sees Jase and me arrive together. Guys whisper and girls scowl. There aren't that many people here, thank goodness. I have no doubt that word will spread like wildfire.

I sent a message to the girls as we left dinner. They are going to head over once the guys are ready.

The football house isn't far from Parker's. At least I know I have somewhere to stay after and can possibly have some drinks.

"Do you want a drink?" Jase asks as he leads me to where the keg is set up.

"Sure, I'll have one." I nod to the red cups that are being filled up.

He grabs two from the table and hands a cup to me. His free hand rests against the small of my back. Warmth spreads over me. Jase is greeted by his football buddies. He introduces me as we go. It's nice to be meeting and making new friends.

"I've got to go sort some things out. Will you be right here for a second?"

"Yeah, sure. You do what you need to." I need a breather. *Where are my friends?* They're never on time—even when they give me a timeframe. They're hopeless.

It's just another party and session of alcohol and making out. I've enjoyed myself, but now we're out in the big, wide world, and I feel out of place. Kind of like I'm the third wheel to Jase and his party guests. *Stupid.* I lean against the doorframe leading into the cleared living space. It's been emptied of everything but two couches. A DJ is set up in the corner with some huge-ass speakers blaring music.

From where I stand, I have a clear view of the front door and the main area. I sip my drink and turn every time I hear someone coming across the porch.

A familiar laugh from the entrance catches my attention. Oh, thank goodness. It's the girls. They step through the door.

"Oi, don't act like a grumpy old man. Get a drink into you and enjoy yourself," Aiden gripes to Dane.

Dane must be in a foul mood, but he looks hot. Jeans sit low on his hips, and he's wearing a button-up, light-blue shirt with the sleeves rolled up. *Drool.*

"There are plenty to choose from in here and around the world. Trust me on that." Aiden winks.

I cringe. Knots twist in my stomach.

Elsie and Addison bounce over to me, looking stellar. They've changed from what they wore to the game. Addison is in jeans and a spaghetti-strap purple top with her long, dark hair, a small wave to it, falling over her shoulders. She always looks amazing no matter what she's wearing. Elsie is in a red dress that fits her curves nicely and rests just above her knees. Her hair is up and out of her face. She could easily be a model. Here I stand—Plain Jane. At least I'm comfortable.

"How did dinner go?" Elsie grins as she slides up beside me. "Tell me everything."

Shrugging, I say, "There's nothing to tell. We ate food and talked." I'm highly aware that Dane is standing with us.

"He better not try anything suspicious," Parker practically growls. "Did you know he came to me and asked if he could take you out?"

This is news to me and, obviously, to everyone else. All heads turn toward him.

"What?" asks Addison.

"Are you serious?" Elsie is next.

Dane's eyes become heated. This is news to him as well.

I tilt my head and stare at Parker. "So, what? Everyone needs your approval?" I snap.

All eyes in the group swing my way. Elsie's and Addison's eyes become wide.

Parker shuffles on his feet, clearly uncomfortable. "It's not like that, Pais," he assures me.

"Well, that's what it sounds like." I have the urge to tip my drink over him. "Just because you're my *big brother* doesn't mean you have a say in who I date. What if I wanted to date one of your friends? Would they need to ask you too?"

"They wouldn't if they knew what was good for them," he grits out.

"Screw you, Parker. I can see whomever I want. I don't

need you dictating who I go on dates with. Pull your head out of your ass." I press the cup to my lips, down the rest of my beer, then turn and storm off.

How dare he? Who the hell does he think he is? My father? Hell, no.

I grab another cup from the table. Turning, I bump into someone. My drink pours over whoever it is. "Damn, I'm so sorry," I rush out.

"It's okay. I can go grab another shirt." Jase chuckles.

My face prickles with heat. Thank goodness it's somewhat dark in here and he can't see my embarrassment. "I'm so sorry. I didn't realize you were right behind me."

He takes my hand, and he pulls me along with him. I'm led right past Dane and the group. All their eyes are on me. Parker's and Dane's are hooded and dark. I smile teasingly. It's mostly aimed at Parker because he's a jerk.

I'm not really taking notice of where we're going. We head up the stairs and along a long hallway. There are four shut doors. Jase doesn't let go of my hand. Instead, he leads me to the farthest door on the right. He pulls me through and closes the door behind me. Only then, he releases my hand. I clasp my fingers together, twisting my ring.

I'm in Jase's room. Is he planning something? My chest tightens with nerves.

My focus remains on Jase. He strolls over to the cupboard, pulling his tee over his head. I'm gifted with the perfect view of his tightly formed six-pack and that defined V. Dane's body is very similar. Here I am, staring at Jase, all the while thinking of Dane. *What is wrong with me?*

I rub my clammy hands over my jeans. "Ah, I can step out if you want me to," I say, though I don't feel confident. A part of me desperately wants to escape back to my friends.

"You're okay. I'm just changing my shirt," he says.

I try to stare at anything but this good-looking, half-naked guy in front of me. Jase's bedroom is tidy. There's a queen-size bed right under the window, a cupboard to the right, and a desk right beside the door where a lamp is turned on. Everything is neat. His bed is even made. What a shock. The guys at Parker's house aren't this tidy unless they're about to have a party. Things start ticking over in my head. Jase is going to try something. What am I going to do to get out of this?

"Do you have a maid?" I blurt out.

He chuckles. He strolls over to me, a shirt clutched in his hand. In the dim light, I stare at his muscles then his features. He grins. My heart races. "No maid here. It's all me and the guys," he says in a low tone—so low that it gives me goosebumps. He stops just in front of me.

My limbs have become jelly. I need to leave. "Oh, okay." I laugh nervously. He takes a step toward me. I move back, and I'm met by the door. I can't go any farther.

"I've had a good time tonight," he says. He still doesn't move—just stands there with his shirt off.

"Me too," I reply honestly. Jase's hand gently glides down my cheek. My first instinct is to run out the door, but I don't want to be rude. Surely Parker wouldn't let me go out with someone who he thought might force himself on me.

"Loosen up, Paislee. I'm not about to jump you. I like you. I'm making that known."

I release the breath I was holding. "Oh, thank goodness. I thought I was going to have to hit you where it hurts."

We both laugh. Jase pulls his shirt over his head.

Relief washes over me. "Look, I want to be honest. I've

just come out of something. I'm not completely ready to jump into anything new."

His blue eyes become soft. "That's okay, Paislee. I'm not out to force you into anything. It may be strange, but I'm not a guy who will pressure a girl." He takes my hand and pulls me into his chest, wrapping his arms securely around me. I feel safe—just like I did in Dane's arms.

We head back down to the party. A huge weight has been taken off my shoulders with my admission to Jase and also his truthfulness. Jase is pulled away by his friend, and I stop at the bottom of the stairs and scan the area, looking for my friends.

I spot Dane first, of course. He's leaning against the doorframe I was when they arrived. I take in his movements. He runs his fingers through his hair, and he hasn't shifted eye contact. He's flirting. I move toward him and notice where his focus is: a blonde girl across the room. She's smiling and playing, twirling her long hair between her fingers. I hate her. She can't have him. He's mine—or *was* mine.

I make my way over to him. "Who are you making googly eyes with?"

His head whips around.

I glance over to the place where he was looking moments ago.

"Who says I was making eyes with anyone?" He raises his brows.

I scoff. "I know you. The hand-through-your-hair play— it's your tell. No one else notices it, but I do. You did it with me. Quite a lot, actually." I laugh, stepping past him and leaning against the wall.

His body turns toward me, and his arm presses against the wall. "Do I now?" His shining eyes meet mine.

The urge to pull his lips to mine is unbelievably strong. I can smell his musk aftershave. Damn, I wish I could kiss him.

I shift my body to mimic his. Now, we face each other. I bring my hand up and start playing with my hair. "You have no idea what that move does to girls. Since you let your hair grow out, it's like a magnet for people like her." I tilt my head in the direction of the group of girls. He shifts his gaze back to where I indicated. They appear to have lost interest in him.

Behind Dane, Aiden and Parker are walking off somewhere. *Perfect*.

My body heats as Dane steps closer. I don't move away like I did with Jase. The music filling the room seems to fade away, and he leans in to my ear. "Did it work on you?"

My breath hitches, and I say, "You have no idea. It's my kryptonite." His hand reaches, and he glides the backs of his fingers down my cheek. Our eyes connect, and I'm lost to him. Nothing and no one else matters but him.

"Pais…" he says in a whisper, causing my stomach to twist. I want him so bad. I crave his touch, his lips.

"Yeah…?" I reply, my voice low. His hand goes to my neck as though he's going to pull me in for a kiss. I want it. Those pink lips call my name.

I'm about to claim him when Addison shows up beside us. He drops his hand and takes a step back. He pulls away from me. My eyes go wide, and his have gone on a wild search of the room. Panic seizes my chest.

"Don't worry. He's out the back," Addison says dryly, disappointment in her tone. That's what happened. He thought Parker was here.

Dane's focus turns to me and Addison. He steps into me, his hand outstretched. "Paislee…"

I flinch and move to put a good distance between us. I pull my lip between my teeth and chew it hard. My chin begins to tremble as he says, "I'm sorry."

I meet his gaze. He's unreadable. "You did it again. This is why we can't be together. You freak the hell out whenever you think Parker is around. You're like a jittery mouse, searching for something, only you don't know what, even when it's right in front of you." I pause. His anxious stare holds mine. "I'm right here. Right in front of you. You're the one who is going to end up with nothing because you are afraid of my brother."

"I'm sorry," he pleads.

I turn and go for the table where the drinks are. I'm ready to drink myself into a coma and forget all about what I had with Dane. It's officially over.

CHAPTER
Eleven

"Are you alright?" Addison moves in beside me while I stand at the table and down my third cup. I'm going to need something stronger. My eyes burn into Dane's back as he leaves the room.

"I miss him. Why can't he see what's in front of him and say, *'Screw it. I want you. Be mine?'*" I clench my fists. A hot flush washes over my skin as anger pulses within me.

Addison pulls me into her arms, and I step back. I don't want sympathy. I'm not even sure what I'm feeling. I want to hate him. I want to love him. My heart is being torn in every direction.

"It's okay. Sometimes people are blind until… they can't have it anymore. That's what's happening with Dane. He wants you more now that he can't or won't have you."

Addison releases her grip on me and steps back. Her eyes soften.

"I know you're right. I'm just not sure how to let go, though."

Addison hooks her arm through mine. Her lips are pulled into a wicked grin. "Let's drink and be merry. Where are the strong drinks? Beer does nothing for me." She drags me along with her until we find all the spirits in the kitchen on the countertop.

I lean against it and wait for her to hand me some concoction. "Where's Aiden, Parker, and Elsie?" I ask, looking around at the other houseguests.

"I think they went through to the backyard. I told them I was coming to find you. Here." She hands me a cup with pink liquid sloshing inside. I'm not sure this is a smart idea. This looks like pure stuff—the kind of drink that would turn you upside down and make you forget what happened the next day.

"Am I going to remember anything tomorrow?"

Addison laughs as she takes a sip of her own pink drink. Her entire body shivers. "Do you want to remember?"

Her question makes me think. I don't plan on getting in bed with anyone, and I'm here with a group of friends.

"Bring it on." I tip my head back and take a mouthful. It burns the entire way down. I'm thankful for the big meal I had earlier. At least I won't be an easy drunk.

"There's my girl." We hit our cups together and go find the rest of the group.

"Oh, my goodness. Jase asked you out?" I laugh, taking another sip of a drink.

Elsie, Addison, and I have found a couch and planted our asses firmly here. The girl I saw Dane flirting with earlier tried to come sit with us. Elsie told her to get lost. I've never seen someone scurry away so fast.

Hiccup.

"Yep. He loved me," Addison slurs. I glance at my phone, attempting to read the time.

"He wouldn't want to love you. That's my job." Parker sits on the armrest of the couch.

"Oh, don't get your underwear in a twist." I laugh then follow it up with a loud burp.

"And you call yourself a lady. You remind me of my sister." Aiden jumps in on the conversation. He sits on the other armrest near Elsie.

I've planted myself in the middle. "I came here with Jase, and I haven't seen him in a while. Should I be worried?" I scan the room for his large frame. "Hell, I haven't even seen Dane." Not since I walked away from him earlier in the night. "My goodness, I don't even know what time it is. I can't read my watch."

All three of us girls burst out laughing.

"It's three a.m., and I think Dane went home. He wasn't feeling the party. If you ask me, he hasn't been himself for the last two weeks." Soberness washes over me with what Parker has said.

"He seems fine to me," I say nonchalantly, trying not to give away my interest in this topic.

Parker turns toward all of us. "It's as if he's come out of a relationship."

I swallow the lump that erupts in my throat.

"He's been moody, snapping at me and the other guys at training. His head hasn't been in the last two games." He shrugs.

A silence falls over the rest of us. I have no words. Has he really been like that?

"I've not seen anything," Elsie chimes in. "Don't you think you would notice if he had a girlfriend? He'd be with her all the time."

I see what she's doing—trying to move the conversation away and basically insinuate that Parker is imagining things.

He takes another pull on his beer, then answers, "Yeah, maybe. Perhaps it's time we get out of here. Can you girls walk?"

"I think I'm going to have trouble," Addison says, giving Parker a seductive stare.

A grin spreads across his face. "I'm sure I can help you."

We pull ourselves off the couch and exit the party. "Should I have gone looking for Jase? Oh, I'm a terrible date. I'd make a crappy girlfriend. I'd ditch my boyfriend." I giggle. My feet stumble before a hand reaches for me—it's Aiden. He has one arm wrapped around Elsie's waist and has caught me with his other hand before I face-planted into the sidewalk.

"Don't worry. He won't hold it against you. He'll probably ask you on another date," Addison says slowly, as though she's focusing really hard on what she's trying to say.

"How are you guys not drunk? You always had a drink in your hands," Elsie asks, glancing between the men.

Parker shakes his head. "I saw you making the drinks and told Aiden that we needed to slow down. I know what you're like drunk. I can't say I enjoy seeing my sister in this state, but at least I'm here to keep an eye on her." He gives me a pointed look.

I smile sweetly.

We walk up to Parker's front door. He unlocks it and we

file in. No words are spoken. Everyone goes their separate ways. I guess I'll find my own place to sleep.

Kicking my shoes off, I stumble into the kitchen and grab a bottle of water from the fridge door. I drink half of it in one go. After screwing the top back on, I undo my jeans and then think better of it. There's a house full of guys, including my brother. They probably don't want to see me in my underwear.

I'll do the next best thing. Since we're friends and all now, surely he won't mind.

I tiptoe past Parker's door and move on to Dane's. Without knocking, I open it. His familiar musky scent hits me in the face.

I walk into the pitch-black room and strip my jeans off. With my arms extended, I search for the bed. When my hands touch the soft mattress, I begin crawling up it. When my hand lands on his warm, bare chest, I pause. A swarm of butterflies takes over my stomach.

A hand lashes out and grips mine, and I squeak.

"What are you doing?" Dane's gravelly voice causes my heart to skip a beat.

I keep going until I've crawled under the covers. He hasn't moved. I shuffle closer. The need to be near him takes over. "Why did you leave the party?" I whisper.

He sighs. "Just wasn't feeling it."

"Wasn't feeling it, or didn't want to be around me?"

His body moves, and his gaze is now on me, his eyes shining. "Both."

My hand automatically glides up his smooth, bare chest and rests on his cheek.

"I miss you," he says, emotion thick in his words.

I shouldn't want him this much. It's probably the

alcohol. I can't help it—my body wants what it wants. Not sure if I'll regret this or not, I lift my head and lean into him. My lips find his. He doesn't push me away. Instead, his arms wrap around my small frame. Our breaths become heavy, just like the kiss.

Dane pulls me on top of him. I'd known I missed him, but this is a whole new level of missing him. I'd craved his touch earlier, and now I can't get enough.

My hands rake through his hair. He groans. I press myself against him.

His mouth moves along my shoulder. "I've wanted this all night. It's all I could think about." He whispers each word between a kiss.

I can't lie. "Me too."

He flips us and I'm under him. His hands run along my bare thighs. Everything aches for him. I wrap my arms around his chest and squeeze.

If this happens, I'm not sure I'll be able to let him go.

"Wait."

His hands and mouth stop, even though I don't want them to. "What's wrong?"

"What does this mean?"

He's silent a moment before saying, "What do you mean?"

"If we let this happen between us, where does that leave us? Am I still going to be your dirty little secret, or are you going to talk to Parker?"

"Paislee…"

In that single word, he gives me my answer. I unwillingly move out from under him. "Look, do you mind if I stay here tonight? I just want to be near you." A weight has taken residence on my chest. I have the urge to cry. I won't, though.

"Sure." His body moves and he lies back beside me.

I reach out and take his hand in mine. I need his touch. "I'm glad Parker has a good friend like you." The words tremble as I speak them. He says nothing but squeezes my hand.

My heart aches as if it's breaking all over again. No more words are exchanged. A simple touch is all I'm allowed.

CHAPTER
Twelve

I groan. My head is pounding as if I've been hit by a bus or whacked in the head by a baseball bat a few too many times. I move a little, and it makes it worse.

"Feeling sore and sorry for yourself?"

My eyes open wide at the sound of Parker. I bolt upright and regret it instantly. "What? Where am I?"

"That's a good question I'd like answered." There's a hardness in his tone.

When I finally manage to focus, even with the throbbing in my head, it becomes clear I'm in Dane's room. *Oh crap.* My eyes quickly fall to my body.

Whew… thank goodness I'm dressed.

Rubbing my forehead, I turn to find an empty spot beside me. "Where am I? I have a black hole in my head. I can't remember what happened toward the end of the night.

I blame your girlfriend." I groan. It's possible I might be sick. My stomach heaves and then subsides. I clutch it.

"You do realize you're in Dane's bed?"

I frown. There was some kissing involved, but I stopped it. Not that I'm about to admit what happened to Parker. I meet his glare. Those familiar eyes are tight, and the pop-out vein is making an appearance. "Where is Dane?" I ask.

Parker sighs. "I came out of my room and found him asleep on the sofa bed. I got curious because that's where you were supposed to be. I went searching and what do I find? You in his bed."

"Parker, I don't even recall anything that happened after Addison fed me all those drinks. Hell, what happened to Jase? I was there with him. Damn…" I bite my lip. It was always going to be bad if or when Parker caught me in Dane's bed. But Dane obviously thought ahead last night. Did he leave right after I fell asleep? Shame fills me. I hang my head to hide it from my brother.

"Perhaps don't drink like that again." He grabs the door handle and turns to leave. "Paislee, I'm only looking out for you."

"Yeah, yeah. Perhaps it's time you let me make my own choices instead of you continually dictating what I do and who I can or can't date." My head snaps up, and I narrow my eyes. "Just because you're my big brother, doesn't mean you run my life. You're not my dad." The second the words leave my mouth, I know I've gone too far. I brought up our father.

Parker whirls around. "I'm nothing like him. Don't ever mention him to me again," he growls. I pull back. His head drops. "Sorry. That man is nothing to me. If he can't be bothered to stay with his family and be a father, then I don't want to be compared to him. You're right—I'm not your dad. I'm your brother, and I've looked out for you your whole life. Which is more than I can say for our father." He turns and leaves, shutting the door behind him. I'm left reeling.

I don't know anything about my dad except that he left when I was a couple of months old. I've never asked about him, and it's very rare that I bring him up. I shouldn't have said that to Parker. He's been my protector my entire life.

I fall back on the pillow before reaching behind me and pulling it up and over my face. I feel like trash. My stomach keeps heaving. My head hurts, and now I've hurt Parker. I'm not even sure I should talk to Dane.

There's a noise at the door. It opens and shuts again. I sense someone in here.

"What? Have you come back for round two?" I speak into the pillow as it muffles my words.

"I want a different kind of round two."

I lift the pillow, and now Dane stands where Parker was a moment ago—he is still shirtless and sporting some serious bed hair. It's sexy. I want to touch him. "Gee, you had everything planned, didn't you?"

"I was prepared for anything, even this situation." He points at me in the bed, a smug expression on his face. Bending over, he picks up my jeans.

I groan. "I have a couple of blank spots in my mind from last night. We didn't…" I wave a hand between us.

He hangs his head. "No, you shut that down pretty quick—which was probably for the best."

Was it really, though? I'm going to have to end whatever it is I have with Jase. Dane still owns my heart, and I'm not sure I'm ready to move on. "Oh, okay. Did you stay all night out on the sofa bed?"

He moves toward the side of the bed I'm lying in. I shuffle over and he sits. "After you fell asleep, I set an early alarm. When it went off, I made my way out there. About an hour later, Parker came out and hit me with my pillow—pretty much growled at me about sleeping with you."

I move the pillow and sit up, making sure to keep my underwear covered by the blanket.

Dane hands me my jeans. "I wonder what he'd do if he found out we've already been together." He grins.

"Probably kick me out." I laugh.

Dane opens his other hand, and there are two little pills. "Figured you might need these."

I take them willingly. I do need them. Hopefully, they stop the pounding in my head.

He leans over and opens the door on the bedside table. There's a small fridge hiding in there.

My jaw drops. "Are you serious? This has been here the whole time?"

"Yep." He gets a bottle of water out and hands it to me.

I put the two little tablets in my mouth and gulp down a few mouthfuls of water. "Thanks for having a backup plan." I reach over and place my hand on his leg. He doesn't hesitate. He takes it and lifts it to his lips. My stomach tightens. I move closer. Lifting my hands, I take his face in them and pull his lips to my own. My body trembles. I know I shouldn't. I want one last kiss. One last touch. One final taste.

His tongue moves with mine, and I'm lost in him. Minutes pass and he pulls back. My chest rises and falls with my heavy breaths.

No words need to be spoken. I drag myself out of bed and pull on my pants. "The feelings I have for you far outweigh my brother's opinion. I lo—" I stop myself. His head comes up, and I'm staring into haunted eyes.

"Pais…" He stands. I straighten. He reaches for me. I hold my hand up, and he pauses.

"Don't make this any harder. I shouldn't have done what I did last night. It was a mistake." I grab my bottle of water and move around him.

"When it comes to you, nothing is a mistake," he says.

I take the door handle and pull to open, walking away once again.

CHAPTER
Thirteen

"Are you telling me you didn't *sleep*-sleep with him?"

"No, I didn't. We slept in the same bed, and there was some kissing and touching, but nothing more. I put a stop to it."

It's been three days since I walked out of Dane's room. I didn't run into any of the girls, so I walked across the road to campus parking and got in my car. Later, back in my dorm, I slept the rest of the weekend away with a massive headache.

"What about Jase?" Addison queries.

"Well, that's an interesting topic. He messaged me the day after the party, saying sorry he didn't follow up with me. He saw I was with you guys, and he let me be. I hadn't heard from him again until today."

Addison, Elsie, and I sit in their apartment, feeding our

faces with all the sugary goodness from their shelf of sugar and drinking some beers.

"What did he say?" Elsie shifts from her spot on the floor to the couch next to me. Addison is stretched out on the carpeted floor.

"First, you need to tell me why you both aren't at the courts."

"We weren't feeling it tonight. I still have a slight headache and am not ready to even consider running around," Addison says.

I couldn't agree more with Addison. I haven't bothered with my runs these last couple of days. I think my heart is still trying to process how it feels. "Alright. Well, Jase has asked me to go on another date with him to the skate night." A night of wearing shoes with wheels on them frightens me. I can't skate, even if my life depended on it.

"Oh, we're going to that as well with the guys," Elsie says before chucking another chocolate in her mouth.

I look between them. "I can't skate."

"That's perfect! It means he can hold your hand and teach you himself." Addison laughs.

My face screws up. "I'm just not sure I like him like that."

As if planned, they both sigh loudly.

"Will you stop saying that? It's only a bit of fun. You can have fun, can't you?" Elsie says.

I nod, still not wanting to go. I wish I could think of an excuse to get out of going, but now that the girls know, they'll make sure I get my butt into gear and show up.

"Message him back while we're with you, and tell him yes." Addison grabs my phone from the coffee table and tosses it into my lap.

I open the messages, still not one hundred percent sure

I want to do it. It's as if I'm betraying Dane, even though that ship has sailed. My eyes flick between the two girls. They're staring at me as though I might do a runner.

Paislee: Hey, I'll go skating with you. Sorry for the late reply.

Reluctantly, I hit send. "There, sent. Happy now?" I show them my reply so they believe me.

They settle back into their spots and nod. My phone pings. Jase's name is on the screen. I open the text.

Jase: That's okay. I look forward to spending more time with you.

I choose not to reply, because I'm not interested in him like that. I shouldn't be pining for Dane, but I can't help it. I want him back.

"I think we should look at a dating app for you." At Elsie's suggestion, I do a double take.

"Are you trying to get me killed? Only stalkers and serial killers go on those to look for unsuspecting victims. I'm sure Parker would have a fit." I cross my legs under me and lean over, taking another Tim Tam from the packet Elsie brought over.

"I've heard more success stories than horrible ones. You can totally pick out the creepers when they want to show you their bits before even having a conversation with you."

This is true. "Sure. But what about Parker?" I raise my eyebrows.

"We won't tell him." Addison shrugs.

"Yeah, I'm sure he'll love that when he finds out," I reply dryly.

Elsie takes my phone.

"Wait, what are you doing?" I leap for my device, but Elsie lifts it higher.

"Downloading an app that I've heard is good."

"No. I'm not ready to date random guys. I think my plate is already full with Dane and Jase."

"Pfft. They're nothing. Well, nothing solid." Elsie rolls her eyes.

I need back up. "Addy, you need to get me out of this," I plead.

"I'm with Elsie. How about when you go on your first date, we come and keep an eye on you from another table?"

"Still doesn't make me feel great." An uneasy tightness lassos around my stomach. Elsie's head is buried in my phone. Her fingers work at the speed of light.

She hands it back. "All done. Now, we wait."

My lips form a thin line. "If something doesn't feel right, then I'm pulling the pin." Both girls nod.

My phone lights up, and the time catches my attention. Seven-thirty. "Damn, I was supposed to go home to have dinner with Mom." I jump off the couch and collect my things. "Sorry, girls. I'll talk to you tomorrow."

We say our goodbyes, and I'm off. I can't believe I forgot. Mom had something she wanted to discuss with me.

My phone rings when I get to my car. It's Mom. "Sorry, Mom, I lost track of time. I'll be home shortly."

"That's okay, honey. Could you stop at the shop and get me something? I've run out of that spicy sauce you and your brother like."

My tongue tingles at the mention of the sauce. It's hot, but the flavor is out of this world. "Yeah, okay. Anything else?"

"Not that I can think of. Thank you. Ah… see you soon."

Something is wrong. She doesn't sound like her usual self. "What's going on, Mom?"

"Oh nothing, honey. It's been a big day at work. See you soon."

Before I can say any more, she hangs up the phone. She's hiding something.

After sliding into my car, I start the engine. My phone pings again. I suck in a deep breath and look at my screen.

Dane: How was your day?

I stare at the screen, puzzled.

Paislee: Was this meant for me?

Dane: Yes it's meant for you. I'm trying out this whole 'friends' thing. I suppose we kind of missed that step.

There goes my heart.

Paislee: Ha ha. I guess that's true. Well, my day was good. I'm heading home to have dinner with Mom. What about you?

Dane: That sounds like fun. So, something just came up on my phone.

A screenshot pops up with the message. It's a picture of my profile on the dating app. I groan. I should have known this would happen.

Paislee: Oh, goodness. You can thank Elsie for that monstrosity. I didn't want any part in it.

Dane: I thought that might be the case. You need to be careful on these things.

Paislee: Elsie and Addison have that covered. They're going to come with me when I go on a date. Hey, wait, what are you doing on the app?

Dane: Keeping my options open. But every girl who's come through is after one thing. There's only one girl I want that way.

Flip goes my stomach.

Paislee: Oh, you're sweet. I'm still going on dates with Jase as well. I kinda feel like a hussy.

Dane: You're a busy girl. You got time in there to catch up with me?

Is he serious?

Paislee: I'll have to check my schedule. LOL.

Dane: Oh that's mean. Ha ha.

Paislee: I'll always have time for you, friend.

I put the phone down and drive off. I stop at the shop and grab what Mom needs. My thoughts are all of Dane.

CHAPTER
Fourteen

When I pull up at home, parking behind Mom, Parker's car is in the driveway, and there's a random dark sedan parked directly out in front. My curiosity is piqued.

I push the front door open. "Mom, I'm sorry I'm late. I got caught talking with a friend," I yell into the somewhat quiet house.

Parker steps out of the living room. His face is hard—no smile there. My stomach drops to the floor.

"What's wrong?" I whisper, dropping my bag under the coatrack by the door.

I pause and listen. A muffled sound—a man's deep voice. "Has Mom got a boyfriend she's introducing us to?"

His lips form a thin line as he shakes his head. "Mom will fill you in. Come on."

I grip the sauce tightly in both hands. I feel sick. *What is going on?*

There's a solemn feeling in Mom's house tonight. It's usually light and full of laughter, even when it's just Mom and Parker here. Tonight, it's as if a bomb is about to go off.

I step around the corner, and Mom's eyes meet mine. Hers are panicked and uneasy. Following her gaze, a man turns in the bench seat I sat in just this morning. I've never met him before. He has short, dark hair and broad shoulders that fill out his suit jacket. He almost looks like an older version of Parker. He stands. He's tall. I thought Parker was tall, but this man is well over six feet. I'm not good at guessing these things.

"Hey, honey. Thanks for stopping and getting that for me." Mom rushes to my side and takes the bottle from my vise grip. She gives me an assuring smile. I don't return it.

"What the hell is going on?" I can't hold back any longer. It feels like I'm walking on eggshells, and I don't like it. I train my gaze on the man once again.

Parker stays beside me. His body is rigid, his hands clenching then releasing on repeat. What if this man is here to cause hurt to my family? I take a hesitant step away from the group.

"Paislee, this…" Mom pauses and swallows. Her shaking hand takes mine. Her entire body trembles. "This is your father."

"What?" My breath seizes. I stare at the man. He gives a weak smile. I see Parker all over him. "Is this some kind of joke?" I laugh nervously. My legs turn to jelly. Mom told me that he left when I was a couple of months old, so I don't remember or know this man. He's a ghost to me. A nothing. A no one.

I back away. My instinct is to run, but Mom has a firm grip on my arm.

"Come on, Pais." Parker's gentle words pull me toward him. He wraps his arm around me and guides me to the couch.

"What's wrong with her?" the ghost says, I guess to my mother.

She doesn't get a chance to answer as Parker's raised voice makes me flinch. "What did you expect? We haven't seen or heard from you in almost nineteen years. Then, you show up and want to know us. Good luck. I don't want anything to do with you," he growls. His face is flaming red. I've never witnessed him so angry. I reach out and take his hand. His eyes fall on mine as they fill with water.

"Parker…" I whisper. He bites his lips together and collapses beside me.

Heavy footsteps head toward us. Mom comes and sits beside me. I'm between two of the strongest people I know. They raised me. They care for me when I'm sick or hurting. They're all I need. They each hold one of my hands. I squeeze them.

"I am sorry about this," the man says.

I don't even know his name. Does he have the same last name as us? I've never asked. I have what I want. Them. That's all I need.

My eyebrows pull together. "Are you really? Why are you here? What is your name?"

His eyes seem to bulge. Even his nostrils flare like a bull's. His pointed glare turns on my mother. "You didn't tell them about their father?"

Mom's mouth opens to respond, but Parker bolts up so fast it scares me. "Why should she? You walked out on your family. Your blood," he yells. Never have I seen him lose his cool with someone. It breaks my heart that he is doing it right now.

"Parker, honey." Mom takes his arm. "Please settle down."

"What do you want?" I find myself asking, not even sure what kind of answer I'm expecting. This man is nothing to me.

His entire demeanor changed when Parker growled at him. He stepped back from him. It wouldn't surprise me if Parker socked him one in the jaw. I might even find it satisfying.

Mom answers for him. "This man is your father, William Kent. He's moved back into town and wants to get to know you both."

"You're joking, right? You're eighteen years too late. I want nothing to do with you." Parker reefs his arm away from Mom. Her eyes are filled with tears. I can only imagine what is going through her head. This man, William, left her, left all of us. My jaw clenches, and red floods my vision.

Standing, I say, "Like Parker said, you're a bit late to the party. We don't need you or want to know you. You had the chance to get to know us throughout our entire lives. And you've happened to move back and realized your family still lives here, so you decide you'd mend those bridges. How dare you?" Bitterness drips from my lips. "You. Are. Nothing. You're not my father. A father would have stayed or at least made an effort to see us." I'm sure I'm repeating myself. I don't care. Perhaps if I say it more and more, he might get it through his head.

William does nothing. He stands tall and listens to what I have to say. All the while, I am torn apart inside.

"Did you tell them about me?" His question is directed to Mom.

This makes me angrier. I step up to him and shove him in the chest. I don't care who the hell he is. "Don't you dare speak to her as though she's done something wrong. She has always told us that if we wanted to know you, all we had to do was ask. Why would we ask, though, when you walked out of our lives and left Mom to fend for herself? You're pathetic. Sorry, Mom. I can't stay here." I turn and walk out of the room.

"Excuse me, young lady…"

"It's Paislee to you," I roar, even surprising myself. I grab my bag and escape through the front door and run toward my car.

"Pais, wait up." Parker's plea brings me to a halt.

"I can't stay here." My words shake. Parker takes my arm and pulls me against his chest. I should be crying, but I've never felt more angry and bitter toward someone. It's as though the flaming red hotness inside me has dried up my tear ducts. "Who does he think he is? Tell Mom I'm sorry. I'll just go back to the girls' dorm." I pull away from him.

"No, go to my place. That's where the girls are heading. I've already texted Addison."

"Okay, thank you." I don't want to talk anymore.

He starts walking back toward the house. I don't think he'll leave until he knows Mom is okay. I should be doing that as well, but my head is swimming with confusion.

There's only one person who will make me feel better. The only person I need is Dane.

CHAPTER
Fifteen

I pull into the college campus car park. It's not a far walk from here to Parker's place. My head is light and all over the place. What person thinks it's okay to show back up in someone's life after zero contact? Did he think we'd be welcoming? Boy, was he wrong. I want nothing to do with him. He's basically dead to me.

I drag my wobbly body out of the car. Each part of me is trembling like never before. I hope Dane is here. I need him.

Time passes, and before I realize it, I'm standing in front of Parker's place. My head is in a world of its own; I didn't notice my surroundings on the walk over here. It's as if something has taken over my body. I find myself moving, but I can't feel my legs doing the work—same with opening the door.

"Is that her?" someone asks. I have no clue who it is. My head swims with thought. I'm in a thick fog.

Addison and Elsie step around the corner, and their features become soft. They're beside me in seconds. Their arms are around me, but I don't feel them or their warmth.

My numb body is led to the couch. "What do you need?"

I turn to the somewhat muffled voice I don't recognize. It's Addison.

"My phone." I don't even recognize my own voice. It's ghostly.

Hands grab my bag from my shoulder, and then something is thrust into my palm. With trembling fingers, I begin typing. I need Dane.

It doesn't matter if Parker shows up or what his thoughts are on the matter. There's only one person who can take away this numbness that has spread over my body. I don't feel anything. Nothing. I don't want to have feelings right now. It's all too much. I don't want to acknowledge the man, William. He's no father. No man walks out on his family and has no contact with them. A weak man would do that. A lowlife.

Paislee: Where are you? I need you.

"Can we get you anything?" Elsie's face comes in front of mine. Her mouth continues to move. What is she saying? Her words are muffled. I shake my head in answer to the question she asked.

The vibrating in my hands brings my unfocused eyes to it.

Dane: What's wrong? Where are you?

Paislee: I'm at your place. Please come.

Dane: I'm on my way. Hold on, baby.

Their eyes are on me. I sense them. I can't bring myself to speak. My voice box seems to have swollen up and stopped working. The lump in my throat stops anything trying to escape—at least it still allows me to breathe.

"She hasn't said a word. I'm worried, Parker. She's like a pale statue of Paislee sitting in your living area. What do you want me to do?" Addison asks, concern etched in her words.

What was Parker's answer?

"We'll stay with her until you get here. How are things going there with your dad?"

She hesitates. Even Addison is unsure how to talk to Parker about it. At least they have each other to lean on. I need secure arms around me. I need one person's touch, and I know the moment he arrives, I'll break into a thousand pieces.

"That's no good. I hope your mom is okay. I'm here for you. I'll see you later." Addison kneels in front of my bent legs. I'm sure I haven't moved. I'm waiting for him.

"Everything at home is okay. Parker isn't going to leave your mom alone."

I manage a nod. A silence fills the room. I'm not sure where Aiden is.

"Do you want me to ring someone?"

I swallow. "No…" Before I manage another word, the front door opens in a wild rush. My eyes search the entrance.

Where is he?

Addison stands and moves.

"Where is she?"

The sound of his voice brings the tears I've been holding back right to the surface. Then I see him. His eyes are wide until they land on me, then they soften. Everything and everyone else fades away. He rushes to me before sitting and pulling me onto his lap. I curl into him, and I can't hold back anymore. I sob like my heart has been torn from my chest. It hurts. It aches. With each tear that soaks his shirt, he holds me tighter against him. I am safe.

After what feels like an eternity, my tears are all but dried up, and clear voices fill my ears.

"So, her dad has shown up after all these years?" Dane's chest vibrates as he asks the question.

"Yes, Parker is fuming. He had no idea what he was going home to. He's glad he got there before Paislee."

Dane's arms tighten around me when my name is mentioned. He's my security. He's my strength. He's my everything.

"I don't understand why he showed up now," Dane repeats.

"Because he's working back in town," I croak through a dry throat as I lift my head from Dane's soaked shoulder. All focus turns toward me.

"Oh, Pais, I'm so sorry." Addison rubs my leg. She's seated beside Dane and me.

I look at Dane. His eyes find mine, which I'm sure are bloodshot and puffy. "Thank you for coming," I whisper and lean in and give him a kiss on the cheek. I'd much rather his lips on mine and us lying in bed with his arms around my frame. His support is so powerful for me.

"For you, I'd run a marathon. Hell, I'd even walk over hot coals."

"But you won't talk to Parker," Elsie chimes in. "Ouch, it's true."

Addison must have swatted at her. She's rubbing her

arm, and Addison is giving her a death stare when I look over at them.

"I know. It's different. He's my best friend, and she's his younger sister. It's going to be hard for him to wrap his head around us. Trust me when I say I'm working on it." He stands with me in his arms as though I weigh nothing then places me gently on the couch. I want to dig my fingers into his arms so he won't let me go. I'm afraid that I'll shut down again if our touch disconnects. I don't, though.

"Well, you better work it out fast, because she's still dating."

"Really, you're going to bring that up right now?" Dane almost growls, annoyance in his tone. I reach for his hand and give it a squeeze, but he pulls it away from me. It's as though I've been kicked in the stomach.

Thank you, Elsie, for ruining this moment.

"Elsie, will you stop please? Dane came when I needed him, and that says so much more about his character than talking to Parker. *He came.*"

Elsie's face turns a slight shade of pink. "Sorry."

The room falls silent, and as if on cue, my stomach growls—loudly. I laugh. Then, everyone bursts out laughing. It slices through the thick tension in the room.

"Well, let's order some food. This girl missed out on her dinner tonight." Addison jumps up from her seat and pulls her phone from her back pocket. "I'll give Parker a call and let him know what's going on."

"Can you tell him I'm okay?" I ask.

She smiles. "Sure." She exits the room to make the call.

I reach up and take Dane's hand again. This time he doesn't pull away from me. "Dane... sit down."

He says nothing but takes a seat beside me. Leaning into

him is like coming home after a long holiday. That sense of belonging. Closing my eyes, I drink in the moment. Everything around me fades away. My father. Parker's issues with who I date. The issues between Dane and me.

"What's going on here?"

I bolt upright like I've been shocked by lightning. Parker stands in front of Dane and me. Blood drains from my face. I turn to Dane and then back to Parker. Words evade me. Parker rushes toward Dane, his face molded in anger. His fists are tight in balls, ready to hit his friend.

CHAPTER Sixteen

"Stop. Wait." Addison rushes into the room and puts her body between Parker and Dane. "He was the only one who could calm her and get her out of the ghost-like state she was in."

Parker pauses. Those stone-cold eyes bore into mine as if they're searching for confirmation. I nod.

"Sorry, man. I was only trying to help and offer support." Dane stands, holding his hands out and pulling away from me.

The disconnection is like a slap in the face. I now get a clear picture as to what Dane has been trying to warn me about when it comes to Parker. My brother was ready to hit his own friend.

Parker turns and walks out of the room. Dane peers back to me and shrugs. "I'm sorry," he whispers, pulling his lips into a thin line.

Here I thought we were getting somewhere, getting closer. I was wrong. I'm the idiot who hoped we could make this work. After what I witnessed, there's no hope.

But it's possible Parker overreacted and was only angry because of our father turning up. I need to talk to him.

Standing, I manage to find my balance. Dane reaches for me, but I swat his hand away, shaking my head. I walk down the dimly lit hallway and go to Parker's door. I rap my knuckles twice on the white wood. I don't have to wait long before it's pulled open. His anger is gone and replaced with a pained look. It breaks my heart.

"What?" He practically growls.

I raise my hand and point a finger at him. "Don't." I pause for a moment. His eyes widen. "Don't go treating me like trash. I get that our father's return isn't something you or I should have to deal with, but don't take your anger out on me, or your friends. Pull yourself together," I grit through clenched teeth. I'm not having his temper taken out on me or anyone in this house. That's not how Mom raised us to treat our family or our friends.

Parker's pinched face softens. "I'm sorry, Pais. I've never been so angry as I was coming face-to-face with William, and when I walked in and saw you lying on Dane, that was the final straw."

I hold my hand up. "Stop right there. Dane is a great guy, and if I *was* seeing him, then you wouldn't get a say." Parker's mouth opens, and I quickly continue. "And as for you being angry, I get it. I'm a mixed bag of emotions as well. Can I come in?"

He moves aside, and I make my way to his bed and sit.

"How are you feeling?" He sits beside me.

"I'm okay. I guess a little overwhelmed because I don't know this man. Do you remember him?"

Parker has never brought our father up to me. When I think about it, he was nearly two when he left. Mom fell pregnant with me pretty quickly after she had Parker.

Parker shakes his head, then it drops, and he watches his fidgeting fingers. "No, I don't. That's probably a good thing."

"How is Mom?" This must be so much for her to take on.

"Oh, she's not doing too well. Dad, William—whatever you want to call him—he contacted her out of the blue. He told her that he was setting up a new firm in town and that he'd like to be a part of our lives." I'm sure if Parker could blow smoke out his ears, he would. Even talking about William brings back that pinched, angry look to his face.

"Why did he think we'd be okay with it? I mean, we're adults now, and if we don't want to see him, we don't have to. Do we?"

"You're right."

"What are you going to do?" I ask hesitantly.

Parker shrugs, shaking his head. "I'm too angry to think about wanting to have anything to do with him. He *left* us. He left Mom. I can't let that go so easily. Mom always told me that if I wanted to know him, she would be open. I never had the desire to meet the man and still don't."

I chew my bottom lip. "I completely understand where you're coming from. There is a small part of me that wants to see what he is like. Yes, I don't like what he did to Mom and us, but my emotions are so up in the air at the moment. I think I'll sleep on it and talk to Mom."

He nods and then stands. "I get it."

Silence fills the room. We're both so overwhelmed by the situation. It would be so easy to say something that left one or both of us upset.

"Are you staying here tonight?"

I give him a small smile. "Thanks, but I think I should go home. I'm sure Mom needs me—well, us—right now. We both have what we're feeling to deal with, but Mom's past has suddenly rushed in and pretty much slapped her in the face. She not only has to sort herself out in this situation, but she's got us to worry about too."

Parker runs his hand over his face, releasing a puff of air. "You're so right. I will be the first to admit that I was only thinking of myself tonight. Perhaps we should get together for dinner with her tomorrow and discuss it all."

"Sounds like a great idea. And this time, we won't have the big elephant, William, in the room—just our family." My lips pull up on one side as I stand. I reach for Parker and tug him into a hug. "We need to support each other, not growl and be angry."

He chuckles. "Agreed."

CHAPTER
Seventeen

"Where are you off to?"

I stop when I hit the bottom of the stairs and turn to Mom. She stands in the doorway. Her hair is tied in a messy bun, and she's wearing sweatpants and a baggy, plain white shirt. This is Mom's casual look.

"Oh, I have a date," I say. I have to stick with the date I've promised Jase. Can't say I'm too keen to be going. I have to tell him I'm not interested in any more dates.

She raises her eyebrows. "Is it with Dane?"

My eyes drop to the floor. "No, that's still not happening. Parker saw us a little too close the other night, and he nearly hit him. And since then, Dane has kept his distance."

When I got home that night, I'd spoken to Mom. She was so confused by our dad turning up.

"I'm sorry, honey. I'm sure there will come a time when Parker will let this issue go. Perhaps I should talk to him."

"No, it's okay. He'll get suspicious about why you're doing it, and that will lead him to me. I'm not ready for that argument, especially if he plans to take it out on Dane. I'll leave it all be right now." I shrug. I wish we could put aside everything and just give it a go for real.

"Paislee, you should go for what you want and not settle for second best."

My chest swells. I have the best mother. She's always so supportive and offers the advice I need to hear. "Thanks, Mom. So, what are you doing tonight?"

She releases a puff of air. "I've got William coming over. He wants to talk."

I don't miss her cold tone. I have no doubt she's bitter toward him, but throughout my entire life, she's never said a mean word about him. I've heard other parents fill their kids' heads with so much hate for the person who left. I can totally understand their reasoning—I'd probably be the same. But Mom's never done that, and she had every right to.

"Why are you even bothering?" I purse my lips.

"Because he wants to know about you and Parker. I think he wants to be given a chance to build a relationship with you both."

"What if he leaves again because he realizes we're not what he wants?"

Mom takes a step toward me. "Paislee, I get it. I really do. I'm trying to give him the benefit of the doubt. A second chance probably wouldn't hurt."

"With you?" I almost yell.

Mom laughs. "Nope. There's no way I would get into a relationship with William again. I want him to know his kids, and I'd like them to not make it difficult." Her lips form a thin line.

Knock, knock, knock...

I turn to the door. I know it's not Jase. I am meeting him at the college. Mom moves past me and twists the doorknob. He's here again. William or Dad, whatever. I'm not even sure what I want to call him yet.

"Hey." Mom's soft voice greets him. I stand there, chewing my lip.

"Hey, sorry I'm late. I got held up at the office." His deep voice vibrates through me. This man is one half of the reason I'm alive. At least I have him to thank for that.

"That's okay. Come in."

William steps into my safe zone, my home. His dark eyes zero in on me. He's wearing a deep-blue suit.

"Hello again." He attempts a smile. It looks strained. I guess I must have a good resting bitch face.

"Hi," I say. My heart is jumping around in my chest.

"Will you be staying?" He holds up a bag of takeaway. I catch the symbol and it's from my favorite Chinese takeaway place. *Damn, he's good.* Mom must have given him a heads up that I was here.

I turn to her. "You stalled me on purpose, didn't you?"

She holds her arms out. "I'm not sure what you're talking about." There it is—that tone she uses when she has done something and is trying to act like she hasn't.

"Oh, you're good."

She smirks. "I've learned a lot from my kids." She leans over and gives me a kiss on the cheek.

William smiles at the exchange. Wow, he totally is an older version of Parker. I'd always thought my brother looked like Mom, but having William in front of me, I can't unsee it now. Parker is him all over, even his height.

"Ah… did I miss something?" William, Dad—*hell, what do I call him?*—turns and shuts the door behind him.

"No, William. Mom is being sneaky as usual," I say.

"You can call me Dad, if you like." He tilts his head.

I think on his response for a split second before saying, "I'll use that when you earn the title." As the words leave my mouth, I inwardly cringe. I've never been so blunt to an adult before. I'm surprised Mom hasn't pulled me up on it just now.

I keep eye contact with him. A small smile touches his lips. "I understand. And you're correct. I do need to earn that title before you use it. Does this mean you'll give me a chance?"

"Maybe." I grin. Mom silently watches the exchange.

"Perhaps we could catch up sometime? I'd like to get to know you."

I suck in a deep breath and nod. "Sure. Sorry, but I have to go now. I'm going to be late for the date I don't want to go on." This response gifts me two puzzled looks, one from Mom and one from William. "Don't worry. He's a nice guy," I assure them. I rush out the door like my butt is on fire. I'm super late now.

Mom silently watches the exchange. There's no doubt she'll be giving herself props for softening me up and bringing us together right about now. But she did make some good points.

"I'm so sorry I'm late." I rush up and grab Jase by the arm. He stands at the entrance to the skating rink.

"Oh, hey. That's okay."

I turn to see who he's standing with. It's some chick I

don't know. A pain throbs in my heart. It shouldn't, because I did come here to tell him I couldn't see him anymore, but him standing here chatting with another girl while waiting for me makes me uneasy.

"Sorry, I didn't mean to interrupt." I release his arm and take a step back.

"Paislee." I face the familiar voice. Elsie, Addison, and the guys walk toward us. There's one person who is missing: Dane.

"Hey, guys," I greet them.

"We've been waiting for you." Addison comes to stand beside me.

"Yeah, sorry. William showed up just as I was about to leave." I take note of Parker. His face tightens at the mention of our father. "Calm your farm, big brother," I say gently. And he does. I don't need another repeat of the other night.

"Hey, Jase," Addison greets. I twist and he is standing directly behind me. All hellos are exchanged, and we make our way inside.

After we get our skates and sit to put them on, my nerves take over. My legs have become like jelly. I turn to Jase who is patiently waiting. "I cannot skate." I chew my bottom lip.

He chuckles. "That's okay. I can help." He winks playfully. I need to tell him where I stand.

"Also, one other thing. Jase, you're a great guy, but I'm…"

"It's okay, Paislee. I know. I saw how you were with Dane at the party the other night."

My jaw drops to the ground with a thud. He saw? Well, who else saw then? "I'm really sorry. I didn't want to lead you on. I'm having fun. How could you tell?" I tug at my laces.

Jase's hand lands on my shoulder. "I'm okay, really. I shouldn't have asked you to come tonight. Truth is, I enjoy your company. You're honest, and I like that. I admire you telling me before things move any further forward." He pauses. For a big burly football player, he's a complete softy. Then he says, "I noticed the closeness and also the tension between you both. I think it was just before you went and started getting drunk."

I bump his shoulder and grin. "You really are a great guy, and I'm sorry about getting drunk. It's not me."

He shrugs, raising his eyebrows. "Ah, you know I already know that. I'm just not the right guy for anyone at the moment."

My stomach twists. If there's one way to tug on a girl's heartstrings, it's that line right there.

"Don't say that. I'm sure the right girl is just around the corner." I stand, already wobbling. "Oh, goodness, this is going to end badly. I can see it now—bruised butt, possible broken wrist or leg. Can you secure me in bubble wrap?"

Jase erupts with laughter.

"I'm serious," I cry.

"Here, let me help." He takes my hands and leads me toward the rink. I grip his hands tightly.

"Don't let me fall, because you'll be coming down with me if I do." There are a number of fellow students here. I'm sure to embarrass myself. Just what I need. I've lost track of Elsie and Addison. At least they can skate. Jase tries to let go of my hand. "Wait, what are you doing?" Panic seizes my limbs, and I drop to the ground, landing squarely on my butt. I suck in a sharp breath. "Dammit."

Jase loses his crap laughing. "Oh, dear. I was trying to put my hands on your waist to guide you. Come on. Up you get." He holds his hands out to me and lifts.

I'm sure the wheels on these things are out to cause me pain. They're the definition of *pain in the ass.*

CHAPTER

Eighteen

Two hours pass and I'm sitting on the side of the rink with an ice pack on my wrist. This was a bad idea. A terrible idea. I had a feeling this was how it would end.

"I think it's just a sprain." Jase lifts my hand and assesses it for the second time.

"Well, that's good." I laugh. He gently puts it down and settles in beside me.

"You really don't have to sit with me. You can go find yourself a girl out there." I point to all the people in the rink and on the chairs around it. "I'm not holding you back. Hell, I even noticed a couple giving me the evil eye."

He smirks. "The only ones giving the evil eye are those I've turned away. I'm not interested in what they want."

Oh, and he's a gentleman. Ladies, we have a winner here.

"I'm sure there are a lot of good ones out there as well."

Jase's arms come behind me. He pulls me against him. "I'm here with you. If you think I'm going to abandon you, you need to think again. Where are the others?"

I scan the rink and spot Elsie, Aiden, Parker, and Addison showing off their skills. I have the urge to throw a ball at them. I lift my good hand and point to them. My phone pings. I remove it from my pocket.

I die a little when I open it. It's from that stupid dating app. I'm going to shut it down—once I figure out how to. Opening it, there's a message from some random guy named Rick.

Rick: Hey, beautiful. I love your picture.

A shiver runs down my spine.

"Who's that?" Jase leans over my shoulder.

"Some creep. Elsie signed me up for this dating app, and I've been getting a few messages like this. There have also been a few who show their bits before striking up conversation. Do you know how to cancel this stuff?"

Jase pulls back and cocks an eyebrow. "Do I look like the type that would go on there?"

I glance between him and my phone. "I don't know. Maybe?" I laugh and I can't stop. Tears fill my eyes.

"Perhaps girls on these things wouldn't be as bad as the ones I meet in real life?" He rubs his chin and purses his lips.

I'm still laughing. "You're killing me here. I reckon girls would be worse on these things. I mean, I could be completely wrong." A sense of lightness falls between us, and I know we're going to be good friends. He's someone I can rely on to have my back.

Jase takes my phone from me. I let him scroll through

the app and my profile. "Have you seen you have ten messages sitting in the inbox of this thing?"

I lean over and have a look. "No, I didn't. I honestly don't want to be a part of it. I'm going to shut it down."

"What if we go through this list and you choose one for you to go on a date with?"

"Pfft, are you kidding me?"

Shaking his head. "Here, look at this guy. He seems nice. There's no *hey, beautiful* or anything."

I read the message.

Callan: Hey, how are you?

"That's just a simple greeting. What if he turns into a creeper and starts sending *those* kinds of pictures?"

Jase chuckles. "Then we delete him and get rid of the app. Fair?"

A slight twist in my stomach makes me second-guess the plan. I glance between the message shining on my phone and Jase. "Fine." I give in.

"Here, write something back." He hands my phone to me. I click on Callan's profile. He looks nice. But what if this is a pretend picture and he is really an older guy who forces girls into trafficking? My head is going places I don't want it to.

Callan has short, neat, dark hair—unlike Dane's. I can't make out the color of his eyes. He seems like a nice guy. He enjoys sports, running, the beach—all things I like.

"What should I write?" I turn to Jase.

"Say hello, silly." He shakes his head. "Do you want something to eat?"

I nod. "Sure, I could eat. I'll have whatever you get." He walks off.

Jase is going to find himself a girl who will take his breath away, and he'll treat her so well.

Paislee: Hi, Callan. I'm good, thanks. How are you?

Even as I type, it feels wrong. All kinds of wrong.

"What ya doin'?" Aiden plants himself in the chair beside me.

"Not feeling great about this dating-app business your girlfriend signed me up to." I can't help the eye roll.

He smiles, shaking his head. "Yeah, she told me about that. You realize you don't have to do it. Just deactivate your account and end it all."

"Well, I can't now. I've agreed to contact this one guy. He looks nice enough, but the whole thing makes me a little uneasy."

Aiden turns his whole body to face me. "If you start talking to this guy, and he comes across as full on, or you're not feeling it, then tell him you're not interested and delete the app." He shrugs. "Simple."

"Yeah, so simple for you. It's not your name and details you're throwing out there," I snap.

He stands, raising his hand. "Don't do it then." He walks away, chuckling. My phone alerts me to another message.

Callan: I'm good. So, tell me about yourself. I'm nineteen, play sports for college, and that's pretty much my life.

Well, he seems genuine enough. I hit reply.

Paislee: I'm eighteen, enjoy sports as well, and I'm at college also.

Callan: Wow, that's awesome. I'd love to meet you in person sometime, if possible. I noticed your hometown isn't far from mine. I'd be happy to drive and come see you, if you're okay with it?

Paislee: Look, this is the first time I've ever used an app like this, and I'll be honest—I'm not ready to meet just yet. I'd rather get to know a little more about you through messages.

Callan: That's okay. I understand. What would you like to know?

Paislee: Tell me about your family?

Callan: Ha ha—family. I'm an only child. My parents are working people—always busy with their own lives. I live on college campus. Play football. Enjoy any kind of sports, really.

Paislee: My brother plays basketball for the college. I enjoy similar things to you. I love hanging out with my friends and having a good time.

"I see your fingers are busy."

If I had a drink, I'd be spitting it across the room. "I could totally take that the wrong way." I laugh.

"Did Callan message you back?" Jase asks.

"Yep. He seems nice enough. He's already asked me to meet with him. I told him not right now. I'm not that silly."

Jase hands me a hot dog smothered in ketchup and mustard.

"How did you know this was my favorite?" I ask, astounded at his choice of food.

"Parker was up there when I was ordering. Lucky, hey?" He takes his seat beside me.

We eat in silence. My thoughts turn to Dane. Where is he? Is he on a date with another girl? I suppose I can't talk. Here I am, sitting with another guy while messaging a third guy about a date. At least Jase and I have been able to discuss things, and he is genuinely okay with it all.

Addison and Elsie are walking toward us. "Hey, are you

staying? Or are you going to come home with us, back to Parker's place?" Elsie asks.

I'll feel guilty if I leave Jase here, considering he's my date.

As though he senses my hesitation, he says, "It's alright. You go with them." He grins reassuringly.

"Are you sure?"

"Yeah. I don't think you'll be doing too much more skating." He nods at my wrist. "I'll message you." He leans over and wraps me in his large arms.

I can't help the quiet sigh I release. He smells damn good, spicy and fresh. "Okay. Thanks for a good night, even though I'm pretty hopeless when it comes to skating." I roll my eyes at the memories of all my falls tonight. Any other girl would probably have been completely embarrassed— not me, though. I cracked up the whole time. Perhaps my concentration lapsed with all the laughing.

We say our goodbyes, and I make my way back to Parker's with my friends.

"How was your night?" Elsie asks while shimmying her hips. "We saw you both getting cozy."

I'm mindful of Parker, who is standing in his kitchen. I catch his arm tensing as he stands at the door of the fridge. Perhaps it's the younger-sister-dating thing that gets him all twitchy. "Look, we're just friends. We've spoken about it, and we're both good with that decision."

"Oh, that's great," Elsie says while sitting on Aiden's lap beside me.

The front door opens, and laugher billows through like a gust of wind. There are two people—a girl and a guy. I'd know his laugh anywhere. Just as I think it, Dane steps around the corner and stops dead in his tracks. His panicked eyes bounce over all of us then pause on me.

CHAPTER
Nineteen

*E*veryone has become deathly silent, except Parker, who is oblivious to the tension that's suddenly filled the room. I've never seen the girl before. She has black hair cut in a short do, like a bob. Thick, dark eyeliner has been traced around her eyes. She's got a slim build. Really, she looks perfect in every way. Even her bright-red lips have me staring at them. Then she smiles. Her short, denim skirt sits way above her knees. She's the complete opposite of me.

I shouldn't be hurt. I've been dating Jase.

Perhaps he's trying to move on. I should let him.

The ache in my chest tells me otherwise. It's as if someone is sitting on my lungs. *Am I even breathing?* I have to be since I haven't passed out yet.

"Hey, what have you been up to?" Parker gives Dane a

sly grin. I know exactly what that one means: 'What have you been up to *with this girl?*'

I should go. I don't think I want to be here for this.

Dane stutters over his words before clearing his throat and starting again. "We've just been down to the beach. Guys, this is Jasmine."

Her lips pull wide, and she lifts her hand before waving to us all. I'm smiling—well, I hope I am. I want to be happy for him. Right now, I'm not sure I can be.

I abruptly stand. All heads swing my way. "Nice to meet you, Jasmine. Well, I'm going to head off."

"I thought you were going to stay?" Parker walks toward the couches from the kitchen.

I chew my bottom lip. What do I say? That I want to be anywhere other than where Dane and *Jasmine* are? "Nah, I messaged Mom and told her I'd be home tonight."

He nods, accepting my lie. "Alright. Also, I'm sorry things didn't work out with you and Jase."

I swipe my hand. "Don't worry about it. I enjoy his company, and we're better off as friends." I give the room a sweet smile and walk out.

I release a loaded breath when I step onto the porch. I want to run. Or maybe hide in a hole and stay there.

I punch my pillow for the hundredth time. Sleep is not my friend tonight. My head is playing a mean trick on me. The moment I shut my eyes, all these images pop into my mind. The main thought I keep having is that Dane has possibly got that girl asleep in his bed, and that's if they're even actually sleeping. I think my heart dies a little at the mental picture.

My phone vibrates on the bedside table. "Who the hell would message me this late?" I mumble. Leaning over, I grab it. It's two in the morning, and Dane's name lights up my phone.

Dane: Are you all right?

I want to yell at him. To scream and let him know that I'm not okay. I don't hate Jasmine. I simply dislike her. I can't hate her, since she hasn't done anything to me. Well, she has, but she doesn't know that.

Paislee: Yep.

Yep, I'm using a short answer because it packs a punch. I could easily go on a date with the guy from the app. That would surely rile Dane up a little more.

I shake my head. Who the hell am I to purposely go out of my way and want to cause Dane hurt? He is only doing what I have been doing—trying to move on.

His response is like lightning.

Dane: I'm sorry about tonight.

Paislee: You have nothing to be sorry about.

As much as I don't want to write that, it's the right thing to say.

Dane: Yes, I do. I hurt you.

Paislee: And I hurt you when I went out with Jase, twice.

Dane: True.

Paislee: How did you meet her?

Dane: We met down at the shore, and we just started hanging out tonight.

Paislee: Is she in your bed right now?

Dane: No.

Paislee: Hmm…

Dane: What's that supposed to mean?

Paislee: Nothing.

Dane: Look, you can't be mad at me. You were just out with Jase tonight.

Paislee: I know that, and I'm trying to be nice here. Jase and I are just friends. He has noticed how you and I are with each other. He knows where my heart is.

Dane: He's a good guy. I wouldn't mind if you did stay with him.

Paislee: It wouldn't feel right to me. It would be forced and that's not me. I miss someone who stole my heart a while ago now. It's complicated.

Dane: I understand. It is. I really thought Parker was going to knock me out the other day.

Paislee: LOL. You and me both. It didn't help that my dad had shown up and thrown our world into a tailspin.

Dane: Yeah, that's crazy. Have you seen him again since?

Paislee: Yes. Tonight, before I went out. He seems nice enough. I can only give him a chance. He's going to have to work harder to tame the beast: Parker.

Dane: That's for sure. Good luck to him. Well, I'm going to try and get some sleep. I miss you, Pais.

Paislee: I miss you too. ILY.

My heart races as I drop the abbreviation for *I love you*. I've never said the words since we were unofficial.

Dane: What does that mean?

Paislee: You'll figure it out eventually.

I grin at my screen. I must look like a fool. He doesn't reply again, and sleep comes so much easier.

I'm sure I go to sleep with a stupid smirk on my face.

CHAPTER
Twenty

Callan: Good morning, beautiful.

I stare at the message. The weekend flew by, and here I am, racing to my first class. I'm too busy looking down, and I smack into a firm body. I stumble back. Strong arms catch mine.

"Whoa, where's the fire?" Jase teases.

"Oh, hey." I steady myself back on my feet, and Jase releases his grip on me.

"Always falling at my feet, I see." He winks. I smack him on the arm. It tenses.

Damn, so firm. "Shut up. You wish I was falling at your feet."

His hand comes to his chest as he cries out in mock pain.

"You're full of it." I hoist my backpack up and start

walking. He slips in beside me and throws his arm over my shoulder. Not even a flutter happens in my stomach.

"How's the app boy going? Did you message him over the weekend?"

"Yeah. He seems alright. Well, he's saying all the right things. He's already started calling me beautiful." I must sound pretty disgusted by that, because Jase pulls me tighter against him.

"You are beautiful, though."

If my heart didn't belong to someone else, I have no doubt I'd still be dating Jase.

Eyes follow Jase and me as we walk the halls to our classes. "You're a smooth talker."

We stop as I've made it to my English class. Jase leans over. He moves in closer. *Is he going to try to kiss me? Abort. Abort.*

Before I manage to move, his soft lips press to my cheek. Then, his warm breath hits my ear. "Well, only we know the truth about our friendship, and if it keeps the groupies away from me, then I'm all for it."

I place my hand on his chest and push him. "You're terrible." I point a finger at him while grinning. "I'm not your deterrent for crazy girls." I shake my head.

"Oh, come on," he teases. His blue eyes shimmer. His short hair is perfectly sculpted in place. Another opposite feature to Dane.

I find myself comparing all guys to Dane more and more. No one has ever come close to him, by my standards.

"Get lost." I walk away from Jase, shaking my head again.

Callan: Are you not talking to me?

I sigh as I read it. I am not interested in this guy. I scrunch my nose up at the message. Alarm bells are already ringing. Yes, he seems nice. But he also comes across as someone who demands attention. It's only been four hours since his last message. Why would he think I'm ignoring him?

A body plops beside me under the large shady tree where I've hidden myself. This spot is my escape. There's only one other person who knows about it, and he's just sat down.

"What's up?" Dane greets. My stomach flips and my heart rate spikes. I sit up a little straighter, taking in his gorgeous appearance. He wears his red basketball shorts with a black tank, showing off his perfectly toned, muscular arms. My safety blankets. I take in the view of him as he leans against the trunk.

My eyes dance around the field in front of us. "Uh, nothing. What are you doing? How's Jasmine going?"

"Don't say her name like it's a bad word." He chuckles.

"Sorry, didn't mean to." I totally meant to. Dane raises his hand and rakes it through his hair. Oh, that move has my insides dancing like a fool. "You're making your move again, are you?"

He turns toward me, his brow pulled down. "What?"

"The hand through the hair. Your signature move." I waggle my eyebrows, shoving him in the shoulder. *Gee, he is solid.* He's more built than Parker, that's for sure, and could drop him easily. He wouldn't, though. Best friends don't hit best friends. And it's always the team first and foremost within the group. The girls support that.

"Whatever you reckon." A small silence settles between us. It's comfortable and peaceful. The birds around us sing their songs and flitter through the tree above us. I hope they don't poop on either of us.

I found this spot after my first day on campus. When I need a moment for myself during or between classes, I come here.

Dane found me here one day after we'd first hooked up. I wasn't sure where we stood with each other. It was here that we decided to keep things quiet and enjoy one another. A small part of me wants to go back to that. Another part wants everyone to know. I want to be able to sing our relationship from the rooftops of the college buildings.

"What brings you here?" I finally break the silence.

His shoulders shrug. "I don't know. I wanted to be near you. Pais… can't we give this another go as a full-blown couple?"

My eyes widen with his question. "What about Parker?"

His head drops and stays there for a second before his shining eyes bore into mine. "Can we deal with him at a later date? I want you back. I want us to be in a relationship. No more of this unofficial stuff. *I want you.* I love you too."

My chest seizes at his proclamation of love. "Are you being serious?" I spin my body to face him. A lump has lodged in my throat. My hand runs over my head. I'm not sure if I want to jump for joy or slink away like I have been to save my feelings. I can't go living in secret again.

He reaches over and takes my hand in his. I take in our locked hands and his face.

"I'm as serious as a heart attack." He grins one of his panty-melting grins.

How does he have this effect on me? I want to climb him like a tree and settle in his arms forever. "So, it will go back to how it was before?"

He sighs. "Only for a short time. I promise. I want you back in my bed. I promise not to push you out this time, and I promise to never push you away again. It's you, always has been."

Leaning over, I press my eager lips to his. His large arms wrap around me, and we topple onto the grass. Both of us break out laughing in the middle of our kiss. Our first kiss in a while. I've missed his lips. His touch. His scent. Everything about him. "So, you figured out what my little code meant?"

"If you think that was hard, you need to try again."

Our faces are inches from each other. I soak up his soft, playful features. The tense lines that had been marring his face have faded. "I'd hoped you'd figure it out. I've desperately wanted to tell you for so long, but I wasn't sure you felt the same way."

"I do and so much more. You're my everything, Paislee. No matter what happens. I'll take all the punches your brother throws at me—although, I hope he doesn't," he jokes.

I smack his chest. I've missed his closeness. It's all I've wanted for the past few weeks.

At least now I know what I'm going to do when it comes to Callan and the stupid app. "So, what are you going to tell Jasmine?" I lay my head on his chest and listen to the rhythm of his heart. It's racing.

"I've already told her that it wasn't going to work out. She's moved on already." He shrugs.

"When are we going to tell Parker?"

There's silence momentarily, then he says, "When he's in a good mood."

I grin at his response.

"Can you come over tonight?"

I nod. "Wild storms couldn't keep me away."

Dane moves and his lips press against my forehead.

This is what I have been waiting for. A white flag has been waved, and the battle that's been going on within me is at peace.

CHAPTER

Twenty One

"You're back together then?" Addison asks as she shoves some of her salad in her mouth.

I nod. "Yep. It's all official. Well, not out-in-the-world official. We still have to tell Parker." Addison and I are at Crabbies, the same place Jase took me for our date.

"What are you going to do about the guy you've been chatting to on the dating app?"

"Tell him I'm off the market and close down the app. I didn't feel comfortable meeting guys that way." I unlock my phone and show Addison the six messages from Callan that are sitting there. I still haven't replied to him.

Her eyebrows shoot up. "He seems pretty aggressive in the way he's contacting you."

"I know. Who says, *'Can you please answer me'* four times?"

The waitress stops by and drops off some water. I

ordered the surf and turf again. It is, once again, mouthwatering. *Dane would love this.*

"I'd be running from that." Addison nods at my phone.

"I couldn't agree more. What should I write back?" I hit the reply button.

> **Paislee:** Hi, Callan. Sorry for the late response—I've been busy. Look, I've also been doing some thinking, and I'm sorry, but I can't let this go any further. Thanks for reaching out to me. I wish you all the best.

I flip the phone toward Addison. She's silent a moment then nods. "Yep, send it. Get rid of that creeper."

I hit send. A huge weight lifts off me when the message goes. I then quickly deactivate my account. "I probably should have waited for his reply before deactivating my account."

Addison laughs. "Probably, but he'll see that you disappeared. Trust me, someone who is messaging like that… you don't need him stalking you. You didn't tell him where you go to school or anything?"

"No, but Elsie put our hometown in there. Do you think I should be worried?"

"Shut up. I'm looking out for you. Not to mention that *army* of ours that's always hanging around."

I swipe my forehead dramatically. "Phew." And then I reach out and touch her arm and say more seriously, "I know you are, and I'm thankful for that."

She takes her glass and drinks half of her water in one go. "Are you going to come to the court tomorrow? It's not our usual night, but I want you to come. I need another girl to help me whoop their asses."

"Yeah, I'm sure all five feet of me is going to make a

difference," I mock, leaning back in my seat to allow my overly full stomach some room.

"Come on. Dane will be there." She dangles the carrot in front of me. How am I supposed to say no to that?

"Fine then, since you gave me a good enough reason. I can easily say that you invited me. Is Elsie going to come?"

Addison shakes her head vigorously. "Hell no. She can't play. For the last couple of weeks, we've tried to include her, but she is hopeless at sports." She waves her hands around dramatically. I can't help but laugh at her dramatics. She's such a clown. She could easily pass for one of those mimes.

"Well, if she does, I don't want her on my team," I respond.

"Trust me, none of us do. Aiden is supposed to be teaching her, but they have more arguments over the rules of the game than they do actual playing time. Aiden loses his cool and then has to walk away. It's pretty hilarious to watch, because five minutes after the heated argument, Aiden is back and then it starts all over again."

I smirk. She is getting her kicks over watching her friend and boyfriend argue over basketball. "You have something seriously wrong with you if you're laughing at your friend's boy troubles."

"Just wait until you see them tomorrow night." Her look is one that says, *just you wait and see.* "How are you going to tell Parker about you and Dane?"

I point my finger at her. "Now that's the million-dollar question. What do you suggest, Oh Keeper of the Happy Parker?" I raise my hands above my head and bow down to her.

She smacks my hand. "What has gotten into you?" she asks incredulously.

"I am floating on cloud nine. Things are going my way, finally. I just have to get over this last hurdle: Parker."

"Be honest with him. He may want to hit Dane."

"Funny you should say that. Dane said he'll take what Parker dishes out to him."

"This is going to be fun."

"Mm-hmm. It is," I say with a grin.

CHAPTER
Twenty Two

All the guys are shirtless and sweaty. I don't want to rub up against my brother or Aiden, but give me Dane's sweaty body any day. My pink singlet is only slightly damp.

Thankfully, Elsie had to work tonight. Although, I would have liked to have seen how she plays.

"Yep, I'm open," I yell out to Parker as he makes his way down the court. His bright red face glances my way.

Addison moves around him, trying to block his play. I catch the massive grin on her face. She's obviously going to do something, but before she can, Parker tosses the ball at me. It slips into my hands easily, and I continue.

I get the ball closer to the hoop. Dane comes out of nowhere. I'm not prepared for him. He moves closer. I shift tactics, turning my back to him and bringing the ball around with my back and butt toward him. He slips in closer and tries to reach around me. His body presses against me. I laugh at his maneuver. "Nice try, buddy." This has been going on our entire game. I catch a glimpse of Parker. I toss him the ball, and he throws it up, sinking it through the hoop.

"Oh, yeah! Who are the champions? We are!" I yell. My hands are in the air, and I do a little dance. "You suck." I point at Dane with a teasing grin.

He shakes his head, giving me a sly grin. "Yeah, yeah. Good game, guys," Dane says as he strides over to where our towels and water bottles sit. I follow. I wish I could attack him—in an affectionate way, of course.

"We totally smashed you guys," Parker says as he walks toward Dane. Addison beams as she trails beside him. Picking up his towel and bottle, he continues, "I'm starving. Let's go cook some food."

We all chime in with our agreement.

Outside, the night air brushes over my damp skin, kissing it with coolness.

"I'm going to get some clothes from my car."

Dane glances my way. I get the feeling he wants to come with me. I shake my head. As much as I'd love for him to, I don't think it's a good idea. We still have to talk to Parker about us.

"I'll come with you." Addison releases her grip on Parker's waist and moves toward me. Her hair is a matted mess, which I'm sure mirrors my own.

"We'll see you guys there," I say.

We go our separate ways.

Addison bumps me in the hip. "I totally saw what was going on with you two. Parker may be blind to it, but I'm not." Her words are playful. She even does a little dance.

"I think we're going to talk to Parker tonight. Are you ready to intervene if needed?"

Earlier today, we'd spoken about Parker, and I'd told Dane that I didn't want to wait forever. I'd already waited well over two months for this.

Addison holds her hand up like she is about to swear in on a court case. "I swear to have your back. He'll probably be angry at first, then he'll eventually let it go. It could take some time."

We make it to my car. I grab my bag of clothes from the trunk.

Lifting my head, that's when I see a dark figure standing in the shadows under the trees of the fence line. A shiver crawls up my spine slowly and then shoots right down to my feet. "Is that a person?" I whisper to Addison, unable to hide the slight panic in my throat.

She turns and looks in the same direction I'm staring. Her body shifts closer to mine. "Is he facing toward us?"

"I think so." I have the urge to run. Scrambling into my car and driving off would be the smart thing to do. "Get in the car. We're going to move closer to the house." The dark shadow doesn't budge.

"What if he's some kind of killer? Shouldn't we report this?" Addison's voice rises with each word. I push the key in and turn the engine over. I press the lock button on the car. At least we're safe in here. I drive out, and as I turn around, I try to shine my headlights where the figure was standing. He is gone.

We both stare at the now-empty spot. "There was someone there. I wasn't dreaming, was I?" I need reassurance that I'm not going crazy. My heart pounds in my chest, and my hands tremble.

"No, you're not dreaming. I saw someone there as well. I'm

going to email campus and let them know there was a strange person on the grounds. That freaked me the hell out."

"Me too," I say breathlessly.

I drive off through the gates and pull into Parker's driveway. This is going to be my designated spot from now on. There's no way I want to run into that figure.

We both jump out of the car and run for the front door.

"Whoa, where's the fire?" Parker spots my car keys. Then, he must notice our panicked faces. "What wrong?"

Dane rushes out from the living room, the struggle evident in his concerned eyes as he fights to hold himself back.

Addison is in Parker's arms. "There was some person standing in the shadows of the campus. It felt like he was looking at us. We couldn't see his face, though." Addison sounds on the verge of tears. I want to cry but manage to pull myself together.

"You need to let the campus security know. I'll ring them." Parker stalks off with Addison tucked safely under his arm.

Dane moves closer. His warm hand clasps my bare arm. I flinch.

"It's okay. It's me." His voice is soothing. I desperately want to bury myself in his chest, inhale his scent, and feel safe. My dark eyes meet his light ones. There's pain in his. He's worried. "It's okay. It's probably some person who lost their way. I'm going to go have a shower." His grip slips to my hand. He squeezes. It's like he's pushing safety and security into me, assuring me that everything is going to be alright.

Things don't feel alright. I don't feel secure or safe. I'm standing in the hallway of my brother's place. I'm running from a shadow, and I'm keeping secrets about the man I love. Secrets, lies, and deception. That's what I'm apparently good at. I've had enough of it. I want to be wrapped in Dane's arms. I want him to restore confidence, like a boyfriend would, that everything will be alright.

Instead of heading to the bathroom, I go straight for Parker, who's in the kitchen with Addison standing close by. Just as I stop in the middle of the area between the kitchen and living area, he says, "I've made security aware. Hopefully, that's the end of it."

I swallow the anxiety clawing its way up my throat. "Dane and I are dating," I blurt. There's no sugarcoating. Nothing.

Parker's eyes widen. Addison's face is shocked. A small smile touches her lips.

"What?" Parker says as though he can't believe what he's hearing.

"Dane and I are seeing each other," I repeat slower. I sense Dane's large frame behind me. "We've been seeing each other for a while now. For the last couple of weeks, we haven't, though, because he ended it because of his friendship with you." My chest vibrates, which makes my words shake.

Parker laughs. "Is this some kind of joke?" He cocks an eyebrow and comes toward Dane and me.

Addison rushes to his side and takes his hand. "I'm happy for you both," she says quietly.

Parker whirls her way, a flash of anger on his face. "Did you know?" he growls.

"I had my suspicions," she lies, and I'm okay with that. I don't want to get her in trouble. "You're not one who takes notice of things like I do."

"Are you kidding me?" he roars. "How could you, Dane? I told you to keep away from my sister. What about the other girl you came back here with the other day? What about Jase?" His red face moves between us. I swallow again.

It's Dane who answers first. "She was nothing. We'd only met that night, and nothing happened. I've spoken to Paislee about it all." He places a hand on my shoulder. It's the strength I didn't realize I needed. Parker's eyes blaze.

I quickly interject. "Jase and I were only ever friends. We both agreed on that pretty early, and I was going on dates with him because Dane ended things between us."

A deathly silence fills the room, a fog of tension seeping in through every crack.

When I can't handle it anymore, I slice through it. "Please don't be mad, Parker. I love him; he makes me happy." I smile. Dane's grip slips off my shoulder. He takes my hand as he moves beside me.

Parker rakes his fingers through his hair and swipes over his face. He releases a low, frustrated growl. "You love him?" he mocks. "You're okay lying to your brother and your friends?" He becomes louder and louder.

"Parker, settle down. Can't you see this as a good thing?"

He turns his incredulous stare on Addison.

"It's okay, Addison. Parker, you need to pull your head out of your ass and accept that I'm eighteen and don't need your *fatherly* consent. So you can rein in the temper." I step toward him, releasing Dane's hand.

Parker pushes me aside and goes straight for his friend. *Thwack*... Parker's fist hits Dane.

"Parker!" Addison and I scream and rush toward him. Both guys roll around on the ground. Dane tries to keep

Parker's hands off him, and Parker is attempting to land another punch. That's when I notice the red seeping from Dane's mouth. His face is bright red as he strains against Parker. But Parker is fueled by anger and I'm guessing some hurt because we kept this from him.

"Parker! Get off him now!" I roar. He's not the only one with a loud voice.

"What the hell?" Aiden yells.

I whip around. "Can you come help?"

Aiden leaps into action and pulls Parker off Dane.

Parker's huffing. He does appear to be hurt.

I bend over and take Dane's hand to help him up. Addison steps forward, offering him a tissue for his lip. It's red, swollen, and weeping with blood.

"Calm down, man," Aiden tries to console Parker.

Red blinds my vision. I turn on my heels, stalk up to Parker, and push Aiden aside. I shove him so hard in the chest it appears to wind him slightly. "How dare you? What kind of brother are you? Tell me this—is Dane a bad person?" I wave in Dane's direction.

Parker hangs his head then shakes it.

I continue, "Do you think he would hurt me?" Again, he shakes his head. "There you have it. Pull yourself together and apologize to him."

"It's okay, Pais. I deserve it," Dane says from behind me.

"No, he owes you an apology. He shouldn't be acting like a damn brute. Say sorry." I push him again.

Parker raises his head. His hard eyes focus on me. "I'm not saying sorry. You both went behind my back."

"What were we supposed to do? You were warning him off me, but even then, it was too late. I watched you walk off and comfort Addison tonight after our little incident, and I realized that Dane couldn't do that for me until we told you. I want him to be my comfort and support like you are for Addison. Is that such a bad thing?"

Parker purses his lips. He might go charging at Dane like a bull again if I'm not careful. I should have thought this through better, but stupid me just went ahead and didn't think about the consequences.

"Paislee, it's not a bad thing. He's my friend. I'm not sure how I feel about you two dating each other. I'm not saying sorry. He deserves what he got for lying to me when he flat out told me he'd keep away from you."

I fold my arms over my chest, releasing a huff. Even a stomp of my foot follows. "Well, you've said your piece now. You're not allowed to have an opinion when it comes to who I date. You got that?" I use the stern voice Mom used to use on us when we were in trouble.

"Fine." He stalks past Dane and me and down the hall.

His bedroom door slams against its frame. I flinch.

CHAPTER
Twenty Three

$\mathcal{E}$ lsie's bewildered gaze shifts between Dane, Addison, and me. "You told him?"

I nod.

She rocks back on her heels, blowing out a low whistle. "Wow," she breathes.

I face Dane, who's cradling a busted lip and a dark bruise that's forming on his right cheek. "I'm so sorry. I did the wrong thing."

Dane laughs, then his face screws up. "Ow." He reaches up and gently touches his face. "No, it's fine. At least now it's out there."

"Sorry." I lean on my tiptoes and press my lips into his soft, warm, unbruised cheek. "At least now I can do this whenever I want," I whisper into his ear. "And I get to stay with you tonight."

"Oh my goodness, is this what we have to put up with now?" Aiden sighs like a little child who has seen his parents kissing.

"Shut up." Dane punches him in the arm.

Addison stands to the side, a small smile on her face, but she can't hide the worry lines that crease her forehead. I walk over to her. "Are you all right?" I open my arms, and she steps into them. "I'm so sorry about this."

"I've only ever seen Parker that angry once before. I'm a little shaken."

I nod. I've heard about her ex-boyfriend, Hayden. He wasn't a great guy.

I release her, step back, and stare her right in the worried eyes. "He is hurt. This is all on me. He would never harm you. Parker is a protector. Go to him. You'll be the one he wants to see."

Her head moves up and down. Guilt spreads through me; this is all my fault. I put that fear in her. "Okay."

I take her hand and walk her down to his door and give it three hard knocks. Seconds later, the door flies open, and grumpy-faced Parker stands there. I tilt my head toward Addison, who I hold against me.

His face softens as he takes her in. His mood shifts. "Little mouse, I'm sorry." He pulls her against his chest. Her near-silent sobs tear me apart.

His eyes meet mine. *"I'm sorry,"* I mouth.

"It's okay," he whispers. I'm not sure if he's talking to me or Addison. I'd rather he soothe her than me.

Things settle down. Parker and Addison don't come out of the room, except to get some plates of the food Aiden has cooked up.

I shove a carrot in my mouth. The flavor tickles my taste buds. "Who taught you to cook?"

"It's called packet mix." He chuckles.

"I should have guessed," I reply dryly then place some noodles in my mouth. This stir-fry is delicious.

My phone starts ringing from my bag that I'd dropped at the front door. After jumping up, I collect it from the pocket. "Hello?" I say without looking at the screen.

"Paislee? It's William," a deep voice announces on the other end of the call.

I go and take my seat back with Dane and the others. "Oh, hey. What's up?" I try to act casual, but damn, the nerves are back. I'm still not sure how to act around him. What if he doesn't like who I've become? Hell, I haven't even decided what it is I want to do when I finish college. I need to make a decision soon so I can pick the right classes.

Papers shuffle from his end. "Nothing. I was calling to see if you wanted to catch up for dinner tomorrow night?"

Even he sounds nervous. I can't begin to imagine what this must feel like for him. When he left, we were in diapers, needing so much care, and now he's trying to fix the wrong decision he made all those years ago.

I think he needs to forgive himself. Even if I forgive him, he's still going to have that guilt over walking away. And I'm not sure Parker will so easily forgive him for what he's done.

"Tomorrow night?" I question, wanting to make sure I've heard correctly.

"Yes. How does seven-thirty sound?"

A tiny part of me wants to say no, but then I'd be just as bad as him. I said I'd give him a chance. "Yeah, okay, seven-thirty sounds good. I'll text you where to pick me up from."

"Oh, you won't be at home?" He sounds shocked and a little let down.

Could he still have feelings for Mom? I'll save those questions for dinner. It'll give us something to talk about. "No, I'll probably be at Parker's place. I'll send you the address." Everyone in the room has gone silent, and all their eyes are on me with questioning looks on their faces.

"Okay, sounds good. I look forward to it. Anywhere in particular you'd like to go?"

"You can choose," I say, then we end the call. I'm met with silence. "What?" I ask, exasperated. It's not like I'm going on a date with another man.

"Who was that?" Dane asks as he places his plate on the floor. Does he even chew his food, or simply inhale it?

"It was William, my dad." I shrug then put more food in my mouth to avoid their questions.

"You're going to dinner with him?" Elsie looks at me with interest.

"Yes, what's the problem? Am I not allowed to get to know my father?" I blurt out in frustration.

Everyone shakes their heads and averts their eyes. My life is like a damn circus at the moment. I'm the tightrope walker. One wrong step and I'll tumble. I'm waiting until I do stumble. At least, if I do, Dane will be there to catch me. As for Parker, I'm not sure. I have to fix what I messed up.

Tomorrow is a new day, and I plan to repair it then.

"Well, I'm going to bed." I pick up Dane's plate and take my own.

"You're stayin'?" Aiden asks, unable to hide his shock.

"Yep, it's all out in the open now. So Parker is just going to have to get over it. Plus, after the little run-in Addison and I had earlier, I'm not sure I want to drive home on my own. I'd rather be here, especially since Mom is working nights again."

Everyone soon goes to their rooms, and the house becomes silent. It's my first night when I'm not having to sneak in the window.

We're official.

No more hiding.

This feels amazing. Excitement ripples through me. I've waited for this moment for what feels like forever. It's finally here.

I brush my teeth and go back to Dane's room. I shut the door behind me before turning around. Dane lies there with his shirt off. A wickedly sexy grin is spread across his face. He taps the empty spot beside him. Slowly, I crawl up him on my hands and knees until we're face to face.

"No more hiding," he says breathlessly.

"Nope," I reply. A surge of excitement explodes inside of me. I lean in and push my lips against his. He tastes like minty-fresh toothpaste. I pull away and bring my legs up so I'm straddling him. My arms wrap around his neck.

Dane's hands press against my back, and he pulls me tightly against him. Our kiss becomes heated, wet, and intense. With each touch, my body ignites with sparks.

Dane is mine. I am his. This is how it's meant to be.

No more hiding. No more secrets.

Everything is how it should be.

CHAPTER
Twenty Four

"Parker, can we talk?" I step into the kitchen as he maneuvers around, cleaning up his mess. He's just made dinner for the house.

"Mmm," is all he says. It's clear he's still angry. Thankfully, he's simmered down—mostly.

I take a seat at the counter and follow his movements. "Parker?"

He stops and looks my way. I'm met with a deadpan stare. "What?" he growls.

"I'm sorry about keeping Dane and me from you. There's something else." My head drops to my fingers, which are strangling each other.

Parker throws his hands in the air dramatically. "Oh my goodness, you're pregnant," he states.

My head shoots up. "What? Hell no. I'm not that stupid." The mere thought of having a baby freaks me the hell out.

"Oh, thank goodness. What do you want, Paislee? Or are you just going to keep apologizing?"

"Will you stop acting like a little child and act your damn age? You do realize I'm an adult. I don't need you behaving like a dictator. You really think I'd go to you and tell you I was pregnant? That's a hard no. I'd let Mom tell you that one. Plus, I'm not a stupid, immature girl." I smack my hand down on the counter.

Parker blinks then folds his arms. "What?" At least this one isn't a growl.

I release a puff of air. "I'm going out with William tonight. He rang me last night and wanted to catch up with me." The words hang in the air, lifeless. I can see Parker's mind ticking over. I'm sure he's contemplating how not to explode, or I could be totally wrong and he's about to flip out once again.

"He rang you?"

I nod.

"And you're going out with him?"

Again, I nod. My chest vibrates as my heart pounds against my rib cage. Parker is being so difficult.

"So, you forgive him for what he did to Mom?"

And there it is. The anger.

"No, I haven't forgiven him. I'm giving him a chance to prove himself to me. To show he really wants to get to know me and plans to actually stay a part of my life." I keep my tone even and try not to rise at his frustration.

"Why are you telling me? You're good at keeping things to yourself." Another sting. It's as though he's cracking a whip across my back, trying to hurt me with everything he says.

"Just stop." I sigh. "Parker, enough with the tantrum. If you don't want me around here anymore, fine. I'll go. It'll be your fault that I'm walking away. Your fault that you can't get your head out of the darkness you've surrounded it in." I don't give him a chance to respond. I hop up and walk out the front. It's nearly time for William to pick me up.

I never in a million years thought I would ever meet my father again. I imagined he was long gone and wanted nothing more to do with my family.

A car horn catches my attention. It's the same car that was parked at Mom's when he first showed up.

I open the passenger door and slide in. It has a new-car smell.

"Hey," William greets me with a massive smile.

"Hey," I say and face forward, chewing my bottom lip. I wish I had asked Dane to come with me, but he had some studying to catch up on in the library.

"I thought Chinese for dinner. Are you okay with that?" William glances over at me before pulling out onto the street.

"Yeah, that's fine with me," I reply.

"How was your day?"

I twist my bag handle in my hands and keep my eyes focused out the window. "Yeah, it was alright. Just the usual."

"Your mother tells me you haven't decided on anything solid to study yet?"

Damnit, Mom.

"Is this the part where you get all fathery on me and tell me what I should be doing?"

He chuckles. "No, I lost that right a long time ago. I would like to talk about it over dinner, though."

Wow, brutal.

"Yeah, sure, we can discuss it. I can't promise it'll help."
I laugh nervously.

The car becomes silent, apart from the radio. I can't help
but wonder what his life has been like without us.

I start making a mental checklist of things to ask. There's
a pile building in my head. I'm not so sure he'll get to discuss
my studies with all my questions.

We get to the small Chinese restaurant and take a seat in
a booth. My focus dances around the room, and I avoid my
father's eyes. I wonder if he's as nervous as me. Mom
probably should have come. She might have split the
tension.

"Why did you leave?" I blurt out then pull my lips
between my teeth. *What the hell did I just say? How stupid am I?*

Before he can answer, a waitress comes over and gives
us a menu each and says she'll be back to take our orders.
Then, it's just us again.

William settles his hands in front of him. His face is
clean-shaven. Dark eyes, dark hair. He's not in the uppity
suit I've seen him in the last two times. Tonight, he's in jeans
and a light-blue polo shirt. Very casual.

"I left because I was stupid. I don't have a good answer
to give you. I was self-centered. Let's just say that. I was
scared about being a dad, and then there was work. I know,
all lame excuses."

He took the words right out of my mouth.

"Okay, let's go with self-centered." I give a weak smile.
"Did you think about us? Think about contacting us?" I
fling the questions at him like he's in.

His eyes soften. "Yes, you and Parker were on my mind.
As for contacting you, I thought it would be better if I

didn't. It might have confused you both, considering I wasn't there when you were little."

"Better for who?" I'm amazed at how calm I'm feeling. I don't hold anger toward this man in front of me. I only want answers any child would.

He nods. "I know what you're getting at—better for me. But also for you and your brother. Look at how you both took it when I showed up now. Imagine if you were younger. Wow, so much more anger."

"Parker is still very angry about you leaving us."

"I know. I have lots of fixing to do when it comes to both you and Parker."

"You got that right." I know the instant it leaves my mouth, I shouldn't have said it. "Sorry."

"That's okay. I deserve it. Actually, I deserve everything you both have to throw at me."

The waitress comes back over with her notepad in her hand. "Ready to order?" She smiles brightly. William and I both order the same meals, and she strolls off.

When William says nothing, the sounds of other people chatting and laughing around us seems to become louder. Noise from the kitchen stoves sizzling away, drinks being poured. My eyes follow the waitress around. Here I am, sitting with my father—something I never thought would happen.

"Did you meet someone else? Like, do you have a girlfriend or new family now?" I hold my breath as I wait for his response.

He puts his cup down. "No, I don't have a girlfriend or another family. Yes, there have been ladies over the years, but sadly, I'm married to my work."

I nod and start breathing again. "That's a little sad."

"It's what I chose." He shrugs, a slight frown on his face.

Our meals show up minutes later. *Now that's quick service.* I take a bite of my honey chicken.

"So, your mom tells me that you haven't actually gotten a job yet?"

I stop chewing and shake my head from side to side.

"How would you feel about coming to work for me a couple of afternoons a week, doing admin stuff?" He raises his eyebrows, hopeful.

I swallow the lump of mushed up food in my mouth. "Are you serious?" I almost yell, shocked at his offer. "Wait, does Mom know you're offering this to me?"

"Yes. She's okay with it. Otherwise, I wouldn't have offered it to you."

I sit up a little straighter in my seat. I want this. I need this job. "Yes. I'll do it."

"You will?" he asks, clearly a little surprised by my quick answer.

"Yes, thank you." I grin. He smiles back.

The night goes off without a hitch. Before I know it, dinner is over, and we're pulling into Parker's at nine.

"Thanks for tonight." Without hesitation, I lean over and pull my dad into a hug.

We still have a lot of mending to do, but I'm so glad he's come back into my life. Perhaps his guidance is what I need to push me in the right direction.

"Oh, that's okay." His warmth spreads through me. I've never experienced the father-daughter-type hug—or relationship. I've watched friends throughout my life talk about their family without even registering I was lacking a parent. It has always been Mom, Parker, and me. Now, William is here, and I want him to stay.

Leaning back, I say, "You're not allowed to go and leave again. You got that? There won't be another chance if you blow this one." I look him dead in the eyes. The interior light in the car is reflected in them.

He takes my hand and squeezes. "I promise you that I'm not going anywhere. And if I have to, you'll be my first call. You have my word." He gives my hand another squeeze.

Truthfulness shines in his eyes. "Okay. Thanks… Dad." I stumble over the last word. It's a new word that I'll have to exercise to get used to. Dad's face scrunches up with a smile, but I catch the glistening in his eyes until he quickly blinks it away. He's such a man—not wanting people to see him all emotional. The only expression men show outwardly is anger.

"I'll be in touch to discuss work."

"Thanks again." I climb out of the car and stand on the curb and wait for him to drive off, then I cross the road to go into the house.

"Well, well, well. You seem to get around, don't you?"

I pause mid-step and turn to the bush lining the fence of Parker's house. "I'm sorry, who are you?"

A figure steps out into the streetlight. It's a skinny guy with dark hair. He wears a singlet which appears torn in spots and a torn-off pair of green cargo pants. "So you move on and forget everyone else. Is this who you are, Paislee?"

My muscles tense at the mention of my name. There's something familiar about this guy. "Callan?"

CHAPTER
Twenty Five

My voice shakes as I say his name. Is it really him or am I in a dream? My legs turn to jelly. We're about four feet away from each other. I could run inside, but it probably wouldn't take much for him to lunge at me.

Please, someone look outside and see me. Please.

"We have a winner here, ladies and gentlemen." He steps toward me.

I freeze when I should be backing the hell away from this creep. My chest tightens.

"You think it's fair to send me that message and delete your account?"

"I'm… I'm sorry. I got back with my boyfriend."

"Who? The old guy in the car?"

"That was my father. Not that it's any of your business." His eyes are dead and lifeless. I see danger there. I have to get out of here. A pulsing begins pumping in my ears. This entire situation is bad. "I think you should leave." As I'm turning to walk away, his hand leaps out and latches to mine like a vise. "Let me go," I growl, trying to pull free. His hold tightens against my struggle.

He takes my other arm and shoves me. I fall. A sharp pain stabs me in the back of the head. A scream rips through the night. It's me. Callan's face hovers over mine.

Someone, please come out.

His hands press against the flesh of my stomach. They sear my skin. I scream. He grabs my upper arms again, then lifts me, and shoves me against the concrete curb harder. Another throbbing pain shoots in my head, and this time, it moves right along my spine.

Opening my eyes, white and colored spots dance in my vision. "Stop. Please," I cry.

"You'll pay for what you did," he threatens in my ear. "You didn't even give me a chance." His breath is hot and dangerous.

I try to wriggle my way out. I jerk my body up and down, trying to dislodge his weight from me. With each move, my head pounds as if it's getting smacked against the ground again. Blackness threatens.

NO! Don't pass out. He can't win.

Tears fill my eyes. Callan's claw-like hands paw my skin as he reaches under my shirt. With each touch, I feel more and more filthy—as though my skin turns dirty in the spots where his fingers press on my flesh.

"Hey!" a familiar voice roars.

The weight that was pressed against me is gone, and I'm light as a feather, floating away, welcoming the darkness that throws itself upon me.

CHAPTER
Twenty Six

Where am I?

A groan pushes through my dry, cracked lips.

"She's awake." I hear my mother's cracked voice, and then there's a light touch on my hand.

Why won't my eyes open?

"It's okay, honey. You're safe." Mom's reassuring voice sends me off into a fitful sleep.

"You need to leave." There's Parker's angry voice again. It's not changed since I last heard him speak.

"She's my girlfriend," Dane says in a tone that means, *I'm not going anywhere.*

Stay, Dane. I want you here. I want to yell it. I want to tell Parker to shut up. Again, blackness takes over.

"Parker, you need to stop acting like this. You're pushing Addison away, your friends…"

"And your sister," I manage to croak out. Finally, my eyes open. Parker and Mom rush to my side.

"How are you feeling, honey?" Mom's warm hand runs up and down my cool arm.

"Like I have a splitting headache. How long have I been here?" I take in the sterilized room. It smells clean. The machine still beeps, but there's one person I want here who's missing. "Where's Dane?"

Parker and Mom exchange a glance. She raises her eyebrows at him. "Parker will answer that question." Mom purses her lips.

"You told him to leave. I heard you. Parker…" I sigh, shaking my head gently. "How about you go, and let him come, because I don't want you here. Your anger is too much for me to handle." I turn away from him and face Mom. Tears brim in her eyes. "I'm okay, Mom."

Parker says nothing and walks out of the room.

"Dane was the one who found that guy hurting you." Her voice cracks, and the tears fall now. A lump forms in my throat when I recall what happened.

"I thought it was him but was too out of it. I'm just glad someone came." My body trembles, and I'm not sure how to stop it.

A hulking figure comes to the door. Mom moves and William steps into the room. "I'm sorry, Paislee. I should have waited for you to go inside." He hangs his head.

"No, Dad, it's not your fault. I did this by getting on one of those dating apps. Never again," I try to joke.

"Paislee, now is not the time for jokes," Mom snaps. Being the doctor that she is, she sets about making herself busy by checking my vitals out as I'm sure she's already done a ton of times since I was admitted.

"How long have I been in here?" I ask again.

Mom sighs and stops what she's filling out on my chart. "Just over twenty-four hours."

"Really? It's only been a day; it feels like forever." I groan.

"I found out about the person who attacked you." Both Mom and I turn to Dad. He continues, "He's a known felon. Has done what he did to you to other women. Now, he'll be charged for his past offenses and the assault on you. I'll make sure he gets buried." His arms are tense as he speaks. He's being the protective father I've always wanted to have. It's nice to have someone other than Mom gushing over me.

"But no more dating apps," Mom chimes in.

"I don't need them anymore. I've got Dane." I smile weakly. Mom hands me a cup with a straw. I sip at the cool liquid.

"Who's this Dane guy? Do I need to give him the dad-slash-lawyer once-over?"

Mom and I laugh.

"No, Dad, he's a good guy," I assure him.

He nods, apparently satisfied with my answer.

"Someone talking about me?"

Mom and Dad move out of my way, and there's my slice of heaven standing in the doorway. Tears instantly fill my eyes.

"Let's go, William." Mom touches his arm, and they both leave.

Dane rushes to my side. "Shh… it's okay. I've got you now. You're safe."

I move over, and he climbs into the hospital bed with me. His arms come around me, and I sob into his chest. All the fear and hurt floods from me and onto his shirt. He holds me tight and doesn't let me go.

"How are you feeling?" Dane asks for the hundredth time.

Rolling my eyes, I say, "I'm fine. I just want to go home."

Mom made them keep me another night to make sure the concussion I'd received didn't eventuate into anything more. I've been told to take it easy, and between Mom, Dad, and Dane, I'm sure everything will be alright. I'll be waited on hand and foot.

"Can I have a minute?"

Glancing around Dane's large frame, Parker stands there, his head low.

"Sure, I'll give you two a moment," Dane says and releases my hand.

"No, wait." Parker holds his hand up. "Wait. I wanted to talk to both of you. To apologize for how I've acted lately. This…" He gestures between us. "… is going to take me a bit to get used to. You're my little sister and he's my best friend. I know I should be happy about it. I guess I've always been your protector, and now I have backup. Not only with Dane, but with William as well."

My chest swells. "Oh, Parker." I stand and walk toward him before I wrap my arms around him. "You'll always be my big brother and protector," I whisper into his ear.

When I release him, he steps up to Dane and extends his hand, and they shake. "Don't go hurting my sister, or there'll be more than one busted lip and a few bruises." He laughs, punching Dane in the arm.

Everything has slowly done a three-sixty, and now we're here. Peace has been made.

"The girls are keen to see you. They're out in the waiting room—they couldn't wait until you came over later." He gives me a sheepish grin.

"Sure, they can come in. I'm hoping to get out of here soon. Then, we can go get something to eat other than this plastic hospital food. I need some real mashed potatoes." We all crack up laughing. Parker leaves the room.

"I knew he'd change his tune eventually," Dane says, and he leans into me, and his lips warm mine.

My hands cup his face. "You knew, huh? Then, why didn't we tell him at the start of all this? Because you were a chicken, that's why." I kiss him again.

"Urgh. No. Don't do that in front of me." My head drops when Parker reappears followed by Aiden, Elsie, and Addison.

"Get used to it," Addison says as she rushes to me and wraps her arms around me tightly.

"Uh… I can't breathe," I say.

She releases her grip. "Sorry." Addison is shoved aside, and Elsie is next with another warm hug.

It's so good having friends like these. Yes, they started out as my brother's friends, but now they're also our family.

CHAPTER
Twenty Seven

A week later

My feet glide with the skates. A couple of weeks ago, I was this hopeless wonder who couldn't get one foot in front of the other. Look at me now. Yes, I move at a snail's pace, but I wouldn't have it any other way.

Someone speeds past me. Lifting my head, I catch the back of Dane. A smile tugs at my lips, and my heart skips a beat. In the brief second I check him out, my skates fumble beneath me. With a thump, I'm on my butt once again. This is about the twentieth time.

"I see nothing has changed." Turning my head toward the voice from my position on the ground, Jase stares down at me, a huge grin on his face.

"Shut up."

He offers me his hand. I take it, and he pulls me to my feet with ease. "So, you and Dane, huh?"

"Yep," I reply, releasing his hand and turning to grip the side of the rink. "How goes the girl hunt?"

He looks away then back to me. "Not so great. I keep getting the groupie girls."

"Yeah, they're pretty bad. Don't worry. I'm sure the right girl is just around the corner. Word of warning—don't do the dating sites. There are crazies on there."

"Yeah, I heard. Sorry about that. I feel like it's somewhat my fault because I pushed you into it."

I swipe my hand. "Don't worry about it. It all worked out."

"But are you alright?" He leans against the rail and holds my gaze.

"I'm okay. Not great, but I'll get better," I answer honestly.

The nightmares have been terrible. Dane has stayed with me every night and woken me from all heart-stopping nightmares. In them, Dane doesn't show up. But then, in reality, Dane's right in front of me, saving me from my hellish dreams.

"I'm here if you need a friend." Jase pulls me in for a hug and actually saves me from falling again.

I burst out laughing. "Sorry."

"What's going on here?" Dane's happy voice chimes in.

"Just stopping her from hitting the ground," Jase offers with a chuckle.

I smack him hard in the chest. Jase takes my hand and guides me into Dane's arms and says goodbye.

"Come on. Let's get out of these skates," Dane says.

"That's the most attractive thing you've said to me all

night." I wink. He shakes his head and guides me off the rink to some seats. "At least tonight I didn't sprain my wrist."

"What am I going to do with you?" He leans and slips off my skates for me.

"Love me."

His heated gaze comes up and meets mine. He kneels in front of me and comes closer. I'm eager for his lips to touch mine. I want to taste him and cherish these moments. I don't have to wait long before his tongue slips between my lips and I'm lost in him.

"I love you so much," Dane says.

Butterflies take flight in my stomach. Dane is everything I need, and I can't wait to see what our future holds.

Would I change how everything played out? No. We needed to take this journey. It's ours. It's special to us. He was once the forbidden fruit I couldn't partake of, and now everything is perfect, and I can have him anytime I want.

The End

Thank you so much for reading My Forbidden Guy. I hope you love Paislee and Dane as much as I do.

Want more? Turn the page for the first chapter in Jase's story. The Right Guy available to purchase here books2read.com/u/3k127O

And come join my reader group Lovelock's Flock facebook.com/groups/742675105787263

To keep up to date with what's happening, sign up for my Newsletter at app.mailerlite.com/webforms/landing/w4c9g7

LIZ LOVELOCK

THE
RIGHT
Guy
MY GUY #4

CHAPTER One

Charity

I can't believe I'm back here again.

Stepping into my old bedroom feels like time has warped, like it's playing some kind of sick joke on me. The smell of musty old things immediately hits my senses. That mold—mixed with some other scent I would rather forget—leeches into me, making me screw up my nose at the disgusting odor that lingers all around me.

White curtains with a lace trim line the windows; only now the trim has browned with age. I quickly walk over, moving them out of the way, and shove the window sash up to let in some fresh air.

As I swing around, I notice the walls are still painted pale pink—well, sort of. The pink has turned into more of an off-pink now, and some of the paint is peeling from the ceiling. Even my original pink bedding from when I was here last is perfectly made on the bed.

That's going to be the first thing I change.

Why did she not update the decor?

My bags drop from my shoulder and fall to the floor with a heavy thud.

Attempting to find something—anything—that will help me connect with this room and my past, I expel a heavy sigh and close my eyes tightly. Panic stabs right through me as anxiety takes hold, while a memory of the way my father's loud, angry voice used to echo through these familiar, yet not-so-familiar, walls.

I release my breath and open my eyes, endeavoring to push thoughts of that man far from my mind.

I didn't have to come here. I could've stayed exactly where I was—in a house that now belongs to me, considering my father has passed away. Only, I want nothing to do with that house anymore. That's why I came here. I need closure because, for years, I waited for my mother to come to me. When she didn't, it left me feeling inadequate. Lacking. Wanting more from a mother who simply wasn't able to provide the motherly love when I needed it the most. And quite frankly, she never fought for me.

They say when parents split, it's the kids who suffer. Well, I most certainly did. I never got to know my mother. My father, a decent man—or so I thought—left with me in tow when I was nine and told me my mother was unfit to take care of me. Now he's gone, and I'm here with her, ten years later, in her home.

This is not exactly how I remember it, and she has a new family now.

A family I didn't know existed.

My father lied to me.

Everything he ever told me about my mom was fabricated. He said she was unfit to care for a child and had not one ounce of motherly love in her body.

When he first took me away, I remember begging him to take me back. I missed my mom. I missed her touch. I remember living in this house, and I know these walls hold the answers to my past and where my life all went wrong.

I waited for the day when Mom would show up at my dad's door to take me back home.

Only, she never came.

I wish I knew all the details of what came to pass, but my father died with his lies, and now I hope my mom can help me discover the truth.

"Are you all settled in?" My mother hovers by the doorway, which makes this whole situation even more uncomfortable than it already is.

Shrugging, I say, "Uh... yeah. Perhaps I need to redecorate." I smile.

She laughs, a hint of nervousness coming through in the tone. "Oh, yes, of course. I didn't want to go ahead with changing anything unless you had a say."

I swallow then reply, "Thanks."

I stare at her as she twists her fingers nervously, an action I am mirroring. My hands freeze and then drop to my sides. The more I look at her, the more I see myself. And the more I see, the more I want to know her. I have a million questions, but not today. Everything is still so raw, like a graze on my knee that stings every time it's touched. Only, this graze is on my heart.

Her shining green eyes are masking a shimmer of tears. "Charity, I *am* sorry about your father. I'm so sorry for failing you. I should have done better." Her voice cracks, and the lump in my throat returns. It seems to be a permanent fixture lately whenever someone brings *him* up. That familiar pain, the agony that stabs me through the heart.

"Mom…" I sigh, unable to form the right words, finally all I can manage is. "Thanks," I don't know this woman. I have no idea whether she knows the pain I have been through.

"Anyway, if there's anything you need, please let me know. Also, I'm not sure what food you like. If you can leave me a list of things you might want, I'll be sure to get them for you from the grocery store." She steps forward. I'm sure she's going in for a hug, but then the mask pulls over her eyes, and she quickly shifts back and exits my room, shutting the door with a quiet click on her way out.

A sigh escapes my tight lungs as I collapse onto the double bed covered in a pink blanket. My body feels as though it's run a marathon, yet I've only been in the car. It was a very stale, silent drive with Mom. She tried to make small talk, but I didn't feel like speaking. Forming a relationship with someone I hardly know is going to take time—and lots of it.

Leaving behind what few friends I had was difficult. People here, in this house and town, are lost memories for me.

There is this one face that's stuck with me over the years, though. His blue eyes were in my dreams for a long time after I left. Jase… my *old* best friend.

Three very light knocks at my door drag me from my thoughts. "Come in," I call. The handle clicks and slowly opens.

Leaning over, I try and see who's there.

Is it Mom?

A young girl pokes her head around, and I sit, welcoming her with a smile.

"Who are you?" she asks without hesitation.

"I'm Charity. Who are you?" I shuffle on my bed and tap it for her to come and sit with me.

In skips a gorgeous little girl, like she doesn't have a care in the world. "I'm Grace. Momma told me you're my big sister. I've always wanted to meet you." She climbs onto my mattress and sits with her legs crossed. Familiar, bright-green eyes like mine, like Mom's, stare back at me. *Sister.* Mom told me about her, but seeing her now is surreal. She's tall, probably comes up to just under my arms, and is wearing the cutest little pink frilly dress with a bow placed perfectly in her hair.

I suck my bottom lip between my teeth and bite. I've never had a sibling. A small amount of anger bubbles inside me toward my dad. Why did he keep so much from me?

"I am your sister. How old are you?"

Grace wriggles up, sitting tall as though she's in a classroom. "I'm seven this year," she says proudly. Her hair is long and dark, like mine, and those questioning eyes burrow a place right into my heart.

"Wow, that's a good age. How are you liking school?" Oh my goodness, I want to know so much about my sister. I've already missed seven years of her life; I don't want to miss a second more.

Dad never met anyone new—well, no one I knew about.

Mostly, I spent my time on my own. Dad never allowed me to have friends over, so I learned quickly that books were my best friends. Every chance I got, I had a new title in hand; of course, they all had to have a happily ever after, simply so I could get the feeling of love. Even if it was just from between the pages of books. Love was something Dad sadly couldn't give me, so I sought it elsewhere.

She rolls her eyes, and I laugh. "School is okay. I like seeing my friends. I don't like my teacher, though. She yells a lot, and it's scary when she does." She pauses a moment. Her head drops and then bounces back up. "I'm glad you're here. Mom has always told me I had an older sister that she hoped I would meet one day."

An overwhelming warmth spreads through my chest. Here I'd thought she'd completely forgotten about me. I was wrong.

"Thank you," I choke out. "I'm glad I get to meet you as well. I hope we can become good friends."

Grace slips off my bed and comes to stand in front of me. She doesn't hold back; instead, she throws her arms around my neck and squeezes. My eyes well up, and a quick tear escapes. She smells like strawberries with a hint of apple. I hold on to her tiny frame and wish for these moments to never stop.

"Ah you're kind of squishing me." Her voice sounds strained. My arms instantly loosen.

"Sorry."

Grace grins. "That's okay. You give good hugs."

I laugh. "So do you." It's as though the crater of emptiness I've been experiencing most of my life has suddenly filled up the moment her arms went around my neck.

She leans back and dances on her toes, clapping her

hands. "I can't wait to show you my room, and I want you to see my favorite park down the road."

"Hey, I might be able to show you a few places. I did some growing up here when I was your age." I wink.

"Oh, that would be fun. Can we go now?" She grips my hand and attempts to pull me off the bed.

Her eagerness is contagious. "Maybe not today. I'm a little tired from traveling, and isn't it close to dinnertime?"

Her shoulders slump. "Okay. Maybe after dinner then?"

"Only if your mom says it's okay," I say. She's a little pushy, this one, but I love her spirit.

She spins on her heel and leaves me to my bowl of emotions. It's a mix between anger over what I was deprived of and sadness that I couldn't see my sister and become her friend sooner. I wish I could have been here for her when she was growing up. Thankfully, she's at a very forgiving stage in life.

Things are going to be different now. I'm here, and I don't plan on going anywhere.

ALSO BY
Liz Lovelock

Lost Series
The Lost One—Book One
The Missing One—Book Two
Lost Series Boxed Set

Letters in Blood Series
Dear Captor—Book One
With Love—Book Two
Forever Yours—Book Three
Dear Captor Boxed Set

My Guy Series
Monday Night Guy—Book One
My Aussie Guy—Book Two
My Forbidden Guy—Book Three
The Right Guy—Book Four
My Guy Series Complete Boxed Set

ALSO BY
Liz Lovelock

ABOUT THE Author

I'm a wife, mother, reader, blogger, and now an author. I'm always busy doing something as I have so much going on, and my three little ones keep me on my toes.

I'm from bright and sunny Queensland, Australia. I have always been a reader. When I was little, I would be up late reading *Garfield* and *Asterix* comic books and also *Footrot Flats*. When I hit high school, they gave us *Tomorrow When the War Began* by John Marsden, and from there my love of books continued to grow.

I keep a notebook and pen beside my bed for when those late-night ideas pop into my head, plus I'm a stationery addict and love pens, notebooks, and, well, anything stationery.

ACKNOWLEDGEMENTS

I'll say sorry first in case I miss anyone.

I'd like to thank my editor—Anna from Creating Ink and to my proofreader, Jenn from Jenn Lockwood Editing. Without you ladies, I'd be thoroughly lost. You've both pushed me with this one. Thank you for fitting me in on short notice and polishing up my work to make it squeaky clean. You're awesome! Thanks for all your advice and guidance.

A huge thank you to Ben from Be Designs for designing the perfect cover and working with me until I was happy. It is everything I wanted it to be. I love it!

Thanks, Reggie Deanching, for a beautiful photograph of Ryan Stacks and Anna Harmon. You're all amazing.

These next mentions are my other halves in the author world. Without their constant support and friendship, I may have given up a long time ago. They're my cyber sisters spread far and wide around Australia and America, so thank you to Jemma Brown aka JB Heller, KE Osborn, Kaylene Osborn, and Belle Brooks. These ladies are truly amazing. I'd be lost without our chats.

To Anastasia—your help has been incredible. Without you and your input, I'd be all over the place.

To my Flock—I love you, girls. Your support is truly nothing short of amazing. I know I have a safe place in my group with you all. Thank you.

To my readers—I feel blessed to have your continuous support. Thank you.

To my family and my husband—you're truly wonderful. You've never given up on me. You sit and listen when I need to vent out my frustrations, never once complaining about it. I love you.

To my three beautiful children—Millie, Cale, and Finn. You three test my patience, but I'm so grateful to have you in my life to love. Families are forever.

CONNECT WITH
Liz online

Check these links for more information about author
Liz Lovelock.

Twitter
twitter.com/LizLovelock

Email
lizlovelockauthor@gmail.com

Website
lizlovelockauthor.com/

Facebook
facebook.com/profile.php?id=100008389321975

Goodreads
goodreads.com/author/show/8268717.Liz_Lovelock

Instagram
instagram.com/lizlovelock/

Or sign up for my **Newsletter**
app.mailerlite.com/webforms/landing/w4c9g7

.